**"Your skin is so soft," he said,
sounding fascinated.
He stroked her breasts a few times
before his fingers zeroed in on
pinching her hard nipples.**

"Ooh." Her head fell back, exposing her long neck.

Hylan recognized an invitation when he saw one and leaned down to plant kisses on the line of her jaw all the way down to her sensitive collarbone. Kissing her was like finding the golden ticket to the chocolate factory. She tasted so damn sweet. What he really longed for was the taste of her caramel-tipped nipples. So much so that his stomach growled with hunger.

Nikki was lost in the magic that Hylan was creating. As far as that little pesky voice in the back of her head, she'd gagged it and locked it in the deep recesses of her mind. All she wanted was for Hylan to keep doing what he was doing. She'd think about the consequences later.

Books by Adrianne Byrd

Kimani Romance

She's My Baby
When Valentines Collide
To Love a Stranger
Two Grooms and a Wedding
Her Lover's Legacy
Sinful Chocolate
Tender to His Touch
Body Heat
Lovers Premiere
My Only Desire

Kimani Arabesque

When You Were Mine
Finding the Right Key
Wishing on a Star
Blue Skies
Feel the Fire
Defenseless
Controversy
Forget Me Not
Love Takes Time
Queen of His Heart

ADRIANNE BYRD

is a national bestselling author who has always preferred to live within the realms of her imagination, where all the men are gorgeous and the women are worth whatever trouble they manage to get into. As an army brat, she traveled throughout Europe and learned to appreciate and value different cultures. Now she calls Georgia home.

Ms. Byrd has been featured in many national publications, including *Today's Black Woman, Upscale* and *Heart and Soul.* She has also won local awards for screenwriting.

In 2006 Adrianne Byrd forged into the world of Street Lit as De'nesha Diamond. In 2008 she jumped into the young-adult arena writing as A. J. Byrd, and she is just hitting the women's fiction scene as Layla Jordan. She plans to continue creating characters that make people smile, laugh and fall in love.

My Only
DESIRE

ADRIANNE BYRD

KIMANI™
ROMANCE

Thanks to all my friends and fans that encourage me every day to keep going. And a special thank you to Brenda Jackson, Tu-Shonda Whitaker and Evette Porter— you each inspire me to be a better writer.

 KIMANI PRESS™

Recycling programs for this product may not exist in your area.

ISBN-13: 978-0-373-86204-7

MY ONLY DESIRE

Copyright © 2011 by Adrianne Byrd

www.kimanipress.com

Printed in U.S.A.

Dear Reader,

I hope that you enjoy *My Only Desire*, book four in the Kappa Psi Kappa series. Taariq and Anna were fun characters to create, and of course it's always a pleasure to revisit all of the other characters in this popular series. And judging by all of the wonderful emails I've received, you enjoy getting to visit with them, too.

The idea for this story sort of hit close to home. I, like a lot of my single girlfriends, have been on my fair share of blind dates and even met some nice Mr. Right Nows. Taariq was a hard nut to crack, but I'm sure that you'll be happy with the results.

I hope you've had a chance to check out the first three books in the series: *Two Grooms and a Wedding, Sinful Chocolate* and *Body Heat*. The fun never stops with these fine frat brothers.

And after reading *My Only Desire,* I hope you will come and visit me at my website www.adriannebyrd.com and drop me a line, or check me out on Facebook.

Adrianne

Back in the Day

Chapter 1

Morehouse College, 1995

Anna Jacobs was already a little tipsy when she arrived at the Kappa Psi Kappa fraternity house. As usual on a Friday night, the place was jam-packed and the music booming from the mega-speakers could be heard three blocks away. It didn't matter. No one complained because they were all either at the party or headed to the party.

After a night of celebrating her passing Mr. Gallagher's brain-crushing calculus class, Anna and her roommate Roxanne decided to check out the frat house that had the reputation on campus for throwing the best parties. Anna was starting to look at the Kappa house as a second home since she and Charlie Masters had become fast friends. It was a *Twilight Zone* phenomenon since Anna wasn't particularly popular and didn't belong to any sorority herself at neighboring Spelman College.

Charlie Masters on the other hand was not only popular,

he was gorgeous—or maybe he was popular *because* he was gorgeous. Then again, most, if not all, the Kappa Psi Kappas were delectable eye candy. And the small crew that Charlie ran with were at the top of the heap.

She waltzed through the frat house door in her itty-bitty black minidress that showcased her long legs and boosted her C-cups so that they looked like double Ds to the casual observer. Men paused and a few women eyed her up and down to determine her threat level. That never really happened to her before, mainly because she normally didn't dress like a hoochie.

Anna's gaze swept across the crowd until she spotted Charlie and his crew in the middle of a step performance in the main room. Everyone was hyped as they watched the complex hand- and foot-work the frat brothers had coordinated for the step show. To Anna there was just something about watching such strong and powerful brothers stomping, yelling and sweating that served as an incredible aphrodisiac—especially Charlie.

She smiled when her eyes landed on him.

Charlie, a tall, golden-skin-toned god with seductive hazel-green eyes was technically just a good friend of hers. But secretly, she'd hoped that one day they could be much more than that. Why not? All the signs were there. Lately, he kept coming up with all these lame excuses to call or come by her dorm the last couple of weeks. Wasn't that a clear sign that he was feeling her?

It was possible. She was reasonably attractive. She wasn't the overtly here-look-at-my-titties kind of attractive like her roommate Roxanne, but more of a conservative-good-girl kind of pretty—except for tonight.

Anna was just shy of six feet with thick, long black hair that hung to the center of her back. Again, it was a rarity that she even wore her hair down. It was usually pulled up into a ponytail and twisted around into a tight bun. But she was hoping this self-made makeover would help her stand out more.

The step-show ended to thunderous applause. Derrick Knight, Randall Jarrett, Charlie Masters, Hylan Dawson, Taariq Bryson and Stanley Patterson all took a deep bow before blending into the crowd for drinks and a few excited ladies.

Stanley Patterson spotted Anna and made a beeline straight for her. She smiled. Stanley was sweet, but was pretty much a tall, goofy redhead. In her opinion he sort of tried too hard to fit in, which she sort of understood, since he stuck out as the only white member of the Kappa Psi Kappa fraternity that she knew of. Anna cut him a little slack because she knew what it was like to be a bit awkward.

"Hey, Anna," Stanley cheesed, sliding his hands into the front of his jeans and shifting his weight from side to side. He had a curious look, especially for a white boy. Sagging pants, gold chains and a box fade haircut that had been out of style for at least three years. "It's good seeing you here tonight."

"Well, you know…I was just passing through," she lied and glanced around. Charlie had disappeared. She stood up on the tips of her toes and scanned the crowd.

"Would you like for me to get you something to drink?" Stanley asked eagerly. "What's your pleasure?"

As usual, Anna didn't have the heart to hurt Stanley's feelings, especially when he looked at her with those large, blue puppy-dog eyes. "Sure, um…I'll just have a rum and coke."

"I'm on it!" He tossed her a wink and then took off like a shot.

"You know that he has the hots for you, don't you?" Charlie said, from behind her.

Anna's smile broadened as she turned on her heels. It

was a miracle that she didn't melt under his green-eyed stare. "You're not jealous, are you?"

Charlie's expression twisted while he pressed a hand against his chest. "Me? Jealous?"

Now he's going to act all innocent.

"Hey, if you like Breadstick we can hook it up."

"Breadstick? Why do you call him Breadstick?"

Charlie chuckled. "Because that's what he looks like—a long, skinny breadstick. That and an older Howdy Doody."

"Minus the freckles," she added.

"So you've noticed. Maybe you *do* like him." Charlie turned up his bottle of beer and drained the rest of it.

"I didn't say that."

"You haven't denied it either." He winked.

Anna folded her arms. The last thing she wanted was for Charlie to think that she had a thing for Stanley. "Then let me officially deny it. Stanley is sweet and all, but—"

"Hey, he's cool." Charlie shrugged. "I know I give him a hard time, but that's my dog. For real. He has a good heart. You'd probably be a good match for him."

Suddenly, she was confused by the mixed signals. *Is he really trying to push me off on his boy?*

Just then a girl with a whole lot of junk in her trunk sauntered by and Charlie did a quick rubberneck for a second look. Miffed, Anna glanced down at her enhanced breasts and tried to push them out a little more.

"I, uh, noticed that you came with your roommate tonight," Charlie added casually. "I thought you two didn't get along?"

Anna's hackles rose. Why was it that lately every time she talked to Charlie, he always brought up Roxanne? Had she totally misread his intentions? Had he been hanging around her in order to get closer to her roommate? "We get along all right," she said, shrugging even though she was slowly starting to feel like a desperate idiot. "We went out to celebrate my acing my calculus test."

"Oh, yeah. I forgot about that." He smiled, causing his dimples to wink at her. "Of course I wasn't worried. You're like the smartest woman I know."

Anna blushed. "I am?"

"I know I wouldn't have been able to get through that French class last quarter without you." He held up his beer bottle in a silent toast.

She shrugged again. "Ah. That was easy. I have family that lives in France. I go there every summer."

"Mmm." He nodded his head while his eyes roamed over her slim figure. Sucking in her flat stomach, Anna pulled her shoulders back so that he could get a good look at all she had to offer. She hoped she measured up. Sure, she was trying to look like some video-ho, but it was only because that was usually the kind of chick that the Kappa men went for. Charlie was no different. He dated the hottest girls on campus. It stood to reason that if she wanted to break out of the friend zone, then she needed to take drastic measures. He never stayed with them for long, but she was sure that she had what it would take to keep his interest.

For a few seconds, they held each other's gaze. Anna wished that she could read his mind, but it was an amazingly hard thing to do. Did he just like her as a friend or was there truly a chance for something more?

"I'm back," Stanley announced, smiling.

Anna quashed the urge to shoo him away and accepted the rum and coke. "Thanks, Stanley."

"Not a problem." He stretched his arm and attempted to brace it against the door frame directly behind her. But instead he missed it completely and went sailing to the floor, taking the coat rack down with him.

Anna and a slew of party-goers jumped out of the way. Stanley landed hard, but surprisingly bounced right back up like a jack-in-the-box. "I'm all right. I'm all right," he announced holding up his hands so that everyone could see for themselves.

A few people snickered and laughed.

"Real smooth, Slick," Charlie said, giving Stanley a playful elbow to the ribs.

"Yo, Charlie." Taariq Bryson threaded his way through the crowd. "Randall and I are about to make a beer run. You want to ride shotgun?" His eyes swung toward Anna. He lifted a curious brow and smiled. "Well, well. I didn't know that you were…busy." His gaze caressed Anna's tall frame as if she was standing there naked. Embarrassment flushed her cheeks while Anna's gaze shifted from Charlie's twinkling green eyes to Taariq's smoldering dark ones. There was no need to *try* and guess what was on his mind since pure carnal lust was written over every inch of his handsome face.

The heat Charlie generated was reduced to a candlelit flame compared to the inferno Taariq generated. He was also at least two inches taller than Charlie with a smooth milk chocolate complexion, compared to Charlie's caramel. She loved milk chocolate. Absently, she licked her bottom lip and noticed how his eyes lit up when she did so.

Stanley cleared his throat and put his arm around Anna's shoulder possessively. "Actually, I was hollering at li'l shawty."

Anna's neck swiveled. *Li'l shawty?*

Taariq chuckled. "Oh. Is that right?"

Stanley's chest grew bigger. "Yeah, that's right."

Anna opened her mouth to respond, but Charlie quickly cut her off. "Yo, T. C'mon, man. Let's head out and let Red here handle his business." He winked.

This was getting out of hand.

Stanley held up his fist. "Good looking out, dog."

Charlie exchanged dabs with Stanley while Anna looked

on with horror. *Say something.* But what? Stanley looked so proud of himself that she was afraid hurting his undersized ego in front of his boys would be tantamount to kicking a box full of puppies.

"I, uh—"

"Let's go, T," Charlie said and then winked at Stanley and Anna. "And you two, don't do anything that I wouldn't do."

Stanley's chest puffed out even farther. "C'mon, man. You know how I do."

If Anna wasn't mistaken, she would've sworn that she saw a flicker of disappointment in Taariq's eyes. But in the next breath, he said, "You two play it safe."

Stanley waved them off.

Taariq cast another look in Anna's direction and then headed out the front door behind Charlie. The moment he walked out of the fraternity house, her body suddenly seemed to need oxygen. She sucked in a deep breath. But when that didn't steady her nerves, she remembered the drink in her hand and downed its contents in one gulp.

Stanley blinked in stunned silence.

"Ahh. I guess I needed that." Anna handed her empty glass back to him.

"Um. Okay." He cleared his throat. "Would you like another one?"

"No. I'm good," she told him, allowing the awkward silence between them to drift and expand, while everyone else in the frat house was bumping and grinding to Shaggy's "Bombastic." More than a few rocking hips and butts bumped her closer to Stanley, so much so that he got the wrong idea.

"Would you like to dance?" he asked, setting her glass down on a table.

"I don't know. Maybe I should be getting back to my dorm room." She gave her best apologetic smile.

"What? But you just got here." He grabbed her hand. "C'mon. Don't be a party pooper. You can share one dance with me. I swear I won't embarrass you."

Anna dug her heels in a bit, hoping that it would buy her brain enough time to come up with another excuse. It didn't.

"C'mon," Stanley urged again with another tug. "Show me what you're working with." He started popping his hips and surprisingly had pretty good rhythm…for a white boy. "Ah. You didn't think I knew anything about this here, did you?"

Damn. He's a better dancer than I am. The realization made her laugh.

"See? I told you that I wasn't going to embarrass you." He moved in close then busted out a few more slick moves.

A few partiers peeped his style and started pointing and egging him on. After a few dance songs, Anna realized that she was actually starting to have a good time.

The crowd chanted. "Go, white boy! Get busy! It's your birthday! You know it!"

Stanley looked as if he was on top of the world with the adulation. A little later with his confidence sky-high, Stanley decided to make his move and lure Anna into a corner of the crowded house. No sooner did he get her over there did Charlie and Taariq throw open the door, lugging in a keg of beer.

"Everybody ready to get their party on?" Taariq shouted.

The crowd responded with a thunderous, *"Hell, yeah!"*

Someone jacked the music even louder. Anna could barely hear herself think. Oddly enough, her gaze didn't initially stray to Charlie, but looked over to Taariq and his infectious smile. She also noticed that there were at least a dozen or so women smiling and batting their eyelashes at him.

However, Taariq glanced over at her. The heat started up again and her stomach looped into knots as if she was about to bungee jump off the side of Stone Mountain. What the hell was going on with her?

"I'm glad to see that you're having such a good time," Stanley said, handing her another rum and coke.

"Uh? What?" Anna forced her eyes to swing back toward Stanley. Guilt inched up her spine. *It's time,* she told herself. She couldn't continue to give the man false hope. Shakily, she drew in a deep breath. "Stanley, we need to talk."

Instantly, his smile melted. "Uh, oh. That's not a good sign."

"Well, I just think that we need to get a few things cleared up…about you and me."

"*Definitely* not a good sign." He reached for his own beer and took a quick swig. "Let me guess. You don't like me."

"No."

Stanley's shoulders slumped. "Damn. Really?"

"I mean I like you," she rushed to get her foot out of her mouth. "I just don't like you in the way that you want me to." She winced and held her breath, hoping that she didn't completely destroy Stanley's fragile ego. "I mean…I look at you like a brother."

"Oh." He dropped his gaze and stared at his bottle of beer. "A brother. Great."

"I'm so sorry, Stanley." Anna placed her hand on his shoulder. "You're a nice guy."

"Oh, God. Not the nice guy routine," he moaned. "That's starting to be the story of my life."

She cupped the bottom of his chin and tilted it up. "There is nothing wrong with being a nice guy. We just don't have that kind of connection. You know what I mean?"

"You mean like the connection you feel toward Charlie?" He lifted his head and trapped her with his vibrant blue gaze.

"What?"

Stanley shrugged. "I'm not stupid...and I'm damn sure not blind. I've seen how you look at him. All googly-eyed and everything." He shrugged. "I mean a lot of girls like Charlie...and Derrick...and Hylan...and Taariq. Hell. I'm the odd man out."

"Stanley—"

"No. No. It's okay. I'm used to it."

Now she felt like crap. "I'm sorry. But I really feel that there's a girl out there that's going to be perfect for you," Anna comforted even as a horrible thought occurred to her. *Oh, God, if Stanley knows...*

"Don't worry. I don't think Charlie has a clue," Stanley said as if he'd just heard her private thoughts. "He's my dog and everything. But like I said, he's used to women looking at him googly-eyed."

That wasn't comforting. "I'm sorry," she said again. "I hope that we can still be friends?"

Stanley attempted to smile, but it failed miserably.

She felt the need to say something else. But the right words failed her and she was left to just awkwardly watch him drain the rest of his beer.

"Well. Enjoy the rest of the party," Stanley said, avoiding her gaze and then peeling away from her so fast that she didn't have time to stop him.

"Great. Way to go, Anna," she mumbled under her breath, convinced that Stanley was going to hate her forever. She tossed back her second drink and then reminded herself that she had a low tolerance level.

Notorious B.I.G.'s "One More Chance" started thumping from the speakers and everyone threw their hands up and started rocking to the smooth beats. Anna scanned the crowd again, searching for Charlie.

"Now where did he go?" A part of her was aware that she was behaving like the same love-struck puppy Stanley looked like just a few minutes ago, but she couldn't help it. She pushed her way through the crowd that seemed to be growing at a rapid rate. For twenty minutes she combed the house before deciding to give up. The problem now was that she needed to find Roxanne so that they could split. However, the idea of shuffling back through the crowd wasn't appealing—not to mention, she was starting to feel the effects of her two drinks.

Drawing a deep breath, she turned so she could start back through the crowd and accidently stepped on someone's foot. "Oops. Sorry."

Taariq turned his wounded expression toward her. "Damn, baby. Watch where you're wielding those shoes." He softened his rebuke with a smile. "So where are you running off to so fast? This isn't the Dixie Speedway, you know."

Anna blinked up at him. *Damn.* He was even better looking up close. She stepped back, hoping the space would help her pull herself together.

It didn't.

"Let me guess, you're looking for your boy, Stanley?"

"Stanley?" She blinked. "No. Um, Stanley is just a good friend."

Taariq's handsomely groomed brows sprung up in surprise. "Oh. Is that right?" He stretched an arm up and propped it against the wall behind her, effectively forming a human alcove. It was definitely better executed than when Stanley had tried it. "Sooo. Does that mean that you don't have a man?"

Her face warmed. "No. Um, not at the moment."

Taariq moved closer. "Do you want one?"

Damn. He doesn't waste any time. His directness overwhelmed her. "Actually, I just need to find my roommate Roxanne and head out," she said, escaping while she could still think clearly.

Taariq's full lips kicked up into a wicked smile. "Sorry, l'il Ma. I didn't know you scared so easily."

"What? I'm not scared," she bluffed.

"No?" His brows arched while his eyes roamed over her again. It was so intense that Anna swore it was a physical caress.

"If you're not scared, why are you running away? I don't bite…unless you ask me to."

Anna swallowed while her nipples hardened inside her lace bra. As luck would have it, that was the exact moment when his gaze lowered.

"Since I know it's not cold in here that must mean that you're excited to be near me."

Anna's entire body blazed with embarrassment. "Wow. What a big ego you have."

"Everything is big on me, *baby*." He inched closer and glided his finger up the side of her right arm.

Anna gasped at the way her entire arm tingled. The playful glint in Taariq's eyes morphed into something dangerously predatory within a blink. No doubt that if she stood there much longer, he was going to have her legs up around his waist—the crowded party be damned.

She removed his finger from her arm. "Let's get one thing straight—I'm *not* your baby."

"You could be. The night is still young."

Anna rolled her eyes. "I gotta go." She attempted to step around him only for him to grab her wrist and pull her back.

"All right. All right. My bad. I'm sorry. Can we start again?"

She pulled in a deep breath while she actually thought about it. "I…I've got a test…tomorrow," she lied.

Taariq stretched up a dubious brow. "On a Saturday?"

"It's a make-up test," she covered. One look in his eyes and she knew that he wasn't buying it.

Instead of calling her on it, he just hitched up his shoulders and widened his smile. "A rain check then?"

"Yeah. Sure." *Don't hold your breath.*

"All right. I don't need a brick building to fall on my head. You're not interested. I get it." He tried to shrug off the rejection, but she could tell that it was something that he wasn't used to. Then, he dipped his brows together as if suddenly a thought occurred to him. "You're not…?"

"What?"

"You know." Taariq winked as if he'd worked out a missing piece of the puzzle before leaning in close so that his minty breath would warm the side of her face. "You don't bat for the other side, do you?"

Anna's mouth fell open. "What?"

"I mean—I know that sort of thing gets explored with you ladies when you're away at college."

She was dumbfounded. "No. I'm not gay."

The mischievousness returned to his chocolaty gaze. "Good. Then I still have a chance."

Not in this lifetime. Anna, now completely turned off, pushed past him and then shoved her way back through the dancing crowd. She spotted one of the girls that lived two dorms down from hers and headed in that direction. "Hey, have you seen Roxanne anywhere?"

Jade turned, sloshing whatever she had in her plastic cup onto the floor. "What?"

"Roxanne. Have you seen her?"

"Silly, my name isn't Roxanne. It's Jade." She giggled in a drunken stupor. "Roxanne went upstairs a few minutes ago. Don't you even know your own roommate?"

"No, I meant…" Anna waved her comment away. "Oh, never mind." She turned and once again pushed her way through the crowd. Mercifully, she made her way upstairs but was then forced to try to figure out where to search next with there being so many rooms.

That is until she heard Charlie's familiar laugh followed by Roxanne's annoying giggly snort coming from a room directly to her right. From that moment on, she operated more on instinct than actual thought. She moved toward the closed door with her outstretched hand and her heart already breaking. By the time she opened the door and saw Charlie and Roxanne, tearing at each other's clothes, her weak heart had already shattered into a million pieces.

Chapter 2

Big, fat alligator tears swelled in Anna's eyes as she watched Charlie and Roxanne laugh and giggle while they playfully tore at each other's clothes. She didn't understand why they didn't spring apart after having been caught in the middle of the act. But then she realized that her loud screaming was just happening inside her head and they didn't know she stood there like a dummy watching them. When Roxanne pulled Charlie's open mouth toward her exposed breasts, Anna finally uprooted her legs and backed away.

From there, she was vaguely aware of rushing back down the stairs and plowing through the crowd. A shove here, an elbow there, she didn't care who got hurt as long as they got out of her way. But after five minutes, the door seemed to be getting farther away, not closer.

Anna swiped at a few tears only to discover that her entire face was soaking wet. Just great. She was a weeping mess in front of the who's who of Morehouse and Spelman College.

Just hurry up and get out of here!

Anna moved so fast that she clipped someone's leg and was sent sprawling toward the floor. She thrust out her hands, hoping to break her fall, but was surprised when a strong arm wrapped around her waist and jerked her back up as if she was tethered to the end of a bungee cord.

"Whoa there." Taariq laughed, setting her back on her feet. "You know I'm beginning to think that walking isn't your strong suit." He chuckled once, but then the humor melted from his face when he took in her expression. "Hey. What's wrong?" He swiped at one of her tears.

"Nothing," Anna lied, and then tried to shove her way out of his arms.

Problem was that he just tightened them and held her in place. "Look. I might be many things, but blind is definitely not one of them. Tell me what's wrong. Did something happen upstairs? Did someone do something to you?"

"I *said* it's nothing." She shoved again and he reluctantly let her go. It was a good thing, too, because she nearly choked on the sob that was lodged in her throat. Anna could feel hysteria creeping up on her, but she told herself that if she could just get outside for some fresh air that she'd feel better.

Shove. Push. Shove. Push.

The door still seemed so far away. *Stay calm. Keep it together.*

Shove. Push. Shove. Push.

Another sob bubbled up. Finally she stormed out of the house and sucked in a healthy dose of the night's crisp, fresh air. The wind blew across her wet face and cooled her down a couple of degrees. She exhaled and from the corner of her eyes, she caught a few curious stares. *Pull yourself together.* Anna mopped her face dry and then started down the front stairs.

"Yo, Anna. Where are you going?"

Anna glanced up and saw a small ring of girlfriends jog up the stairs.

"Don't tell me that the party is whack," Emmadonna said, settling a hand on her thick hips. "You know how long it took me to get ready for this mess?"

"Three hours," Ivy chirped, irritated. "Not to mention you used up all my hair gel—again."

Emmadonna's neck swiveled. "Damn. I said I'd buy you another jar. You're the one who wanted me to come to this party and you know I couldn't come without getting my finger-wave in tight. Shoot." She patted her rock-hard hair. "I came to get a man tonight."

As usual Emmadonna's sister-girl act put an immediate smile on Anna's face.

"You're always looking for a man," Anna reminded her.

"You can't find what you don't look for. Ain't that right, Ivy?"

"Whatever." Anna shrugged her shoulders.

Emmadonna swiveled her neck and jabbed her other hand onto her hip. "Soooo…did you do it—or did you chicken out? Don't tell me that you chickened out with Charlie tonight."

Anna's jaw clenched.

"You did, didn't you?" Emmadonna rolled her eyes. "Girl, what am I going to do with you? How are you going to get out of this friend zone if you don't tell Charlie that you're feeling him?"

"Look, Em—"

"No. You look." Emmadonna swung her heavy arm around Anna's shoulders and started to lead her back toward the frat house. "That boy is waaay too fine to just keep on your friend list. I know you're feeling him and I seen him look at you."

"He looks at everything with two legs and two breasts," Anna muttered dejectedly.

"Well, there you go! You're his type." Emmadonna laughed. "Now get your butt on in here and—"

Anna dug in her heels and shook her head. "I don't think that's a good idea. I was leaving."

"Leaving?"

"It's just ten-thirty."

"I know. I just…have a lot I…um—"

Emmadonna wasn't trying to hear it. "Girl, if you don't get your butt in here…"

Anna wrenched herself from Emmadonna's hold. "No. I said I'm going home."

Emmadonna gave chase, surprising Anna with her speed and agility when she snatched her by her arm at the bottom of the stairs. "Whoa. What the hell? What happened in there?"

"Nothing," Anna lied. Unfortunately, Emmadonna wasn't buying it.

"Something gotta be wrong with you running out of here with your tail tucked in between your legs. Now spit it out."

More partiers arrived and tried to squeeze their way past the girls. Impatient, Emmadonna tightened her hold on Anna's wrist and then tugged her off to the side. "C'mon, now. We've been best friends for forever. I know you better than you know yourself. What happened?"

At that moment the dam broke. Tears tripped over Anna's lashes and then streaked down her face at a pace that startled her friends.

"Oh, my God. He turned you down," Emmadonna concluded and then pulled Anna into her strong arms for a smothering hug. "I'm so sorry."

Anna's eyes bugged as she struggled to get air into her lungs. When it was clear that was nearing on being impossible, she started whacking her friend on the back in hopes that Emmadonna would catch a clue and release her. She did. Just a mere second before Anna blacked out. Coughing and sucking in air, Anna managed to shake her head.

"Are you going to be all right?" Emmadonna asked, referring to Anna's broken heart and not her possible broken ribs.

"I'll live," she said with mild conviction. "I just want to go."

"What did he say?" Emmadonna insisted. She always went in for the juice. "Do we need to roll up in here and curse his butt out? 'Cause you know I will."

Emmadonna lived to curse people out. Drama was her middle name. "No."

"Humph! I'll be right back." Emmadonna turned.

Anna knew that her protest had been overwritten and that she'd have to confess more than she wanted to in order to stop her well-intentioned friend from getting rowdy. "Charlie didn't say anything."

Now Ivy peered over Emmadonna's shoulder to stare Anna down. "So what happened?"

Anna mopped her face again and wished that the earth would just open and swallow her whole. "He didn't say anything because I didn't tell him. Okay? Now can we just drop it?"

"You punked out?" Ivy asked, frowning. "Damn. Do you need me and Emmadonna here to go in and pass him a note to ask if he likes you? He can check box *yes* or *no*."

Anna huffed in frustration. "Why can't you just leave it alone?"

Emmadonna cocked her head as she read Anna's face easily. "There's another woman."

Jackpot. The two women's gazes clicked as the friends finally read the truth in her face. Frankly, none of them should've been surprised. Charlie was a ladies' man. He'd never hid or denied that. She should have just left well enough alone. They were just friends—so why did she feel so used?

"So, who is the bitch?" Emmadonna challenged as she started to remove her earrings. "Did anybody bring a jar of Vaseline?"

Ivy dug into her purse. "I think I have a small jar."

"It's Roxanne."

They froze.

"Roxanne…as in your roommate? That Roxanne?" Emmadonna checked.

Anna nodded. "So? Do I have your permission to leave now?" She was on the verge of having another tidal wave of tears hit her and she would rather it happen when she was alone. "And since Roxanne was my ride—any chance one of you mind driving?"

"You're not going anywhere," Ivy announced, hip-bumping Emmadonna's plus-size frame out of the way and swinging an arm around Anna's shoulders. "Screw Charlie…and the horse he rode in on."

"Yeah," Emmadonna cosigned, tossing Ivy's jar of Vaseline back into her purse.

"I never liked that weave-o-rific heifer anyway."

A small smile returned to Anna's lips. It was funny to see soft-spoken Ivy get a little feisty on her behalf. "Don't get mad at Roxanne. She doesn't know that I like…liked Charlie in that way."

"Is there something wrong with her eyes?" Emmadonna countered. "Stevie Wonder can see that—"

"Em, please. Just drop it." Anna pinched the bridge of her nose to stave off a massive migraine.

"Come on, girl. We're going back in there." Emmadonna

took one arm and Ivy grabbed hold of the other and together they started marching Anna back into the party.

"What? Wait."

"No waiting. Once you get thrown off a horse, you don't just lie on the ground and wait for another one to just trample all over you."

"Yeah," Ivy said. "You pick yourself up, dust yourself off and get back on that sucker."

"Cowboy metaphors? Really?" Anna twisted her face as she was once again shoved back through the fraternity house. The music seemed ten decibels higher. The bass pulsed in perfect time with the thin vein pounding along her temple. Bumping and grinding bodies made the whole place look like it was just seconds from turning into one mass orgy.

"Hot damn," Emmadonna said, shaking her thick booty. "This is the joint right here!" When she then dropped it down low and then picked it up again, a young brother rolled up on her and tried to show her what he was working with. "I'm going to catch up with you two a little later," she told Anna before drifting away.

Anna stared after her friend, stunned to be abandoned within seconds of entering the party.

"Don't pay her no mind," Ivy consoled. "You know men are her weakness. What *we're* going to do is have ourselves a good time. Charlie Masters is not the only shark in the sea—and the fastest way to get over one man is to get *under* another one."

Anna frowned. "Come again?"

"Girl, that's what my momma told me and she has never steered me wrong."

"Your mother has been married like eight or nine times," Anna reminded her.

"She practices what she preaches—and trust me, every husband is better than the last." Ivy laughed.

"All right. What the hell?" Anna conceded the fight. It was clear that none of her girls were going to let her escape this place so that she could go back to her dorm and cry her eyes out.

"Really?" Ivy checked.

Anna bobbed her head. "Yeah. But I think I need a drink first."

"Then a drink it is!" She snatched Anna by the hand and proceeded to tug her through the throng of people—yet again. In the crowded kitchen, the girl bypassed the beer keg for the harder stuff on the counter. Before Anna knew it, she was tossing back tequila shots like she was on spring break in Cancun. Next thing she knew, the alcohol snuck up on her and started numbing her heartbreak.

Soon all thoughts of Charlie melted away and all that existed was the jamming beats bumping throughout the house. She closed her eyes and started rocking her hips. She was feeling good—damn good.

"Oooh. So you *do* know how to loosen up," an amused baritone said from behind.

Anna turned to see Taariq once again hovering above her. "Of course I do. Don't look so surprised." She lazily ran her fingers through her hair, suddenly fascinated by how soft it was. Yep. She was drunk, but not so much that she didn't catch the way Taariq's gaze tracked her fingers and how a glint of lust had returned to his eyes. Suddenly, Anna's playful smile became flirtatious while her own gaze dragged down Taariq's body. God. Help. Her.

"Tell me something, Taariq. Do you have a girl?"

Next to her, Ivy choked and then sprayed out her drink. Undoubtedly, she was just as surprised as Anna at her boldness.

"No." Taariq moved closer so that his firm chest could brush against her breasts. "I don't have a steady girl." Their eyes were open invitations, ones that they were both eager to accept.

Anna held one last shot in her hand and she tossed that sucker back for a sweet burn before handing the shot glass over to Ivy. "I'll catch up with you later," she whispered with a wink.

Ivy's brows arched while amusement hugged her lips. "Well, all right then, giiirrl. Work it out."

Taariq wrapped an arm around Anna's shoulder and led her back toward the main living room just when TLC's song "Creep" blasted over the crowd.

"Oh. I loooove this song," Anna moaned, shaking her hips and snapping her fingers.

Without missing a beat, Taariq pulled up to her bumper and got in where he fit in. They moved together as if they had been doing so all their lives. But the heat was turned up when Taariq's hands started roaming all over her body. It started low on her legs and then glided up her firm thighs before finally rounding her hips. Everywhere they went, he left a trail of fire that at that moment she was willing to let consume her.

Then everything started to blur. They were laughing and the room was spinning. Not to mention, she was hot as hell and could feel beads of perspiration start to roll down the sides of her face and even drench her neck. Anna did notice that Taariq's chest wasn't the only thing firm on him. He had biceps to die for and huge shoulders that beckoned her to rest her head.

The music changed up and En Vogue's "Something He Can Feel" had everyone grooving a little more sensually. However, in their case, Taariq was the one soliciting all kinds of feelings. For once in her life, she was just going to roll with it. She wasn't going to bog herself down by overthinking every little thing like she usually did. This felt wonderful and she wanted to take things up a notch.

Taariq's hand roamed from around her waist to take a bold position on her apple-shaped booty. When there was no objection, he squeezed—and she moaned. That was a signal for him to move in closer. He inhaled her flowery scent while she nearly overdosed on his seductive cologne. Heaven opened up in her mind and before she knew it, she was floating on thick, fluffy clouds without a care in the world.

"You sure do know how to move," Taariq whispered up against her ear. "Is that a skill you just have on the dance floor or do you know how to move in other places?"

Anna opened her eyes and stared into Taariq's dark lustful gaze. "I've never had any complaints." Of course her list of partners could be added up on two fingers so it wasn't like that qualified her to have a comment box.

"Is that right?" He pulled his full, bottom lip in between his teeth and dropped his gaze to her hypnotic cleavage again. "So what are my chances of finding out?"

Anna turned just when Charlie and Roxanne descended the stairs, giggling and clinging to each other. Their clothes were crumpled and Roxanne's hair looked a hot mess. If it wasn't for the alcohol, Anna's jealousy would've reared up and she would've flew across the room to snatch all that whack-yaki weave out of her head. But for now, she was still floating and enjoying the low simmering fire Taariq's body and hands started across her body.

"I'd say that your chances of seeing all my moves have just increased to a hundred percent," she said sexily.

Surprise lifted his brows, but he wasn't about to wait around on the dance floor on the off chance that she might change her mind. His arm transformed into a hook and he proceeded to direct her toward the stairs—and Charlie and Roxanne.

Anna dug in her heels and then tried to back away.

Given how fast his erection was stretching toward his

knees, Taariq feared a sweet opportunity was about to pass him by when Anna started backing away. "What? What's up?" However, when he glanced down at her, she was still smiling.

"Tell you what. I think I have a better idea," she cooed.

"Oh?" He liked the sound of that. "What do you have in mind?"

She nodded as she moved closer and pressed against him. "How about you take me back to my place?"

Taariq whipped out his car keys and winked. "You ain't said nothing but a word."

Chapter 3

Anna's head was spinning when she climbed into Taariq's black SUV. There was a small voice shouting in the back of her head, asking whether she knew what she was doing. But she drowned out the annoying question by humming Whitney Houston's "Shoop, Shoop." No thinking. No over-analyzing. This was going to be a world better than just crying into her pillow about a secret crush gone south. Much better.

Taariq opened the driver's door and smiled at her as he climbed in next to her. It was amazing how his frame and his presence just filled up the space. It almost took her breath away. She cocked her head and stared at him. How come she had never really noticed him before? The question fumbled in her mind while he put the keys in the ignition. Maybe it was because she'd always seen him just in passing—and then only a couple of times.

"Are you ready?"

Good God. His black gaze was absolutely mesmerizing.

She eased across the seat and lifted his arm and then draped it around her shoulders. "I'm more than ready," she purred with her gaze drifting down to his full lips. Damn. He even had a perfectly shaped mouth. *I wonder what he tastes like*.

No sooner had the thought crossed her mind was she leaning in close, puckering her lips.

Taariq smiled and rolled with it.

Pure chocolate with rum filling. She released a long, winding moan while lifting her hands to cup his handsome face. Jeez. She could drink from his lips for the rest of her life as far as she was concerned. Nothing she had ever tasted had been so rich and decadent. Anna inched closer and moaned louder.

Taariq's arm fell from her shoulders and then looped around her waist. In the next second, his moans mingled with hers. Soon they both forgot about their need for oxygen, they just fed from each other's mouths as if they were each other's manna from heaven.

When Anna couldn't starve her lungs of oxygen any longer, she eased back and gasped for air. "Oh, my. You taste really good." Did she say that right? It kind of sounded slurred to her own ears.

"You're pretty delicious yourself, baby." He winked and finally started up the car.

Instead of easing back over to the passenger side, Anna chose to snuggle up against Taariq's broad shoulders. To her delight they were as strong and comfortable as she had imagined. She sighed and closed her eyes. Even then her head was still spinning like a carousel.

"So where am I going?" Taariq asked.

"Spelman dorms," she murmured and then gave her building number. She shifted a bit, but only so that she could sink further into the crook of his arm. Once she found her spot, she was in heaven.

"Are you all right?"

"Uh, hmm." She sighed. "I'm just getting comfortable."

"All right." He chuckled and then pressed a kiss against the top of her head.

Aww. How sweet. She slid her arms around his waist like he was her favorite teddy bear. No doubt if she wasn't slightly liquored up at this moment she would've thought her being all hugged up with a guy that she hardly knew was highly inappropriate. Her parents raised her with more sense than this. It was just...well, it just felt right to be where she was. Especially after what's-his-name broke her heart tonight.

What was his name again? Anna frowned as she tried to get her brain to rifle through her mental Rolodex. *Charlie.* The name finally floated upward, but it didn't give her anything close to the feeling she was experiencing right now with Taariq.

While Anna marinated on that thought for a moment, she could feel the vehicle roll to a stop. A second later the engine shut off.

"Anna?" Another kiss was pressed to her head before there was a gentle shake to arouse her. "Are you awake, baby?"

"Hmm?"

"We're here," Taariq murmured softly and then waited for her response. When he didn't get one, he shook her again. "Baby?"

Anna moaned and then stretched. When her thick fan of lashes opened, she drank in his handsome features. "Hey," she moaned as if waking up to him was completely normal.

Taariq chuckled softly as he shook his head. "Hey, yourself. So you think that you can walk up to your dorm room or should I carry you?"

She snuggled closer. "Like if we were on our honeymoon?"

"Uh…oookay," Taariq hedged. "Exactly how much did you drink tonight?"

Anna rolled her eyes while her smile slid wider. "Oh, I don't know. A couple?"

His laughter deepened. "Just a couple?"

"Something like that." She twirled a finger in her hair as she finally pulled herself out from underneath his arm. "Should we go up?"

Taariq's brows arched upward. "Do you think that you can make it?"

She frowned at the silly question. "What do you mean? I'm fine."

He gave her a dubious look but then pulled the keys out of the ignition and climbed out of the car. Since she was practically in his seat, he offered a hand to help her out from his side, as well.

"Whoo," Anna said, almost tumbling. Something must be wrong with her legs and why was the street moving?

Taariq kept an arm wrapped around her waist. "Are you sure that you're okay?"

Anna righted herself by clinging to him. "Yeah. Never better." She giggled for a moment and then became fixated on his mouth again. His perfect…luscious…mouth. She lifted her finger and then lazily brushed it across the bottom. "I want to kiss you again," she whispered.

Still highly amused, Taariq laughed while he maneuvered to shut the SUV door behind her.

"Mmm-hmm." She bobbed her head like a little girl.

"You're adorable, do you know that?"

Her smile melted as she dropped her gaze. "Adorable… but not beautiful." The thought disheartened her. That was probably the main reason what's-his-name preferred Roxanne over her. She was and would always be the plain

Jane with the brains. Suddenly Anna felt like a joke. She glanced down at her tight attire and felt a wave of embarrassment wash over her.

Taariq took hold of her chin and lifted it until their eyes met. "You're both. Beautiful and adorable." He kissed the tip of her nose. "I'm sure you already knew that."

Anna shook her head even though his gaze only reflected truth. *He really believes that.* Her smile returned and as a reward Taariq lowered his head and pulled her soft lips in for a kiss. Her body slumped against him while every troubled thought she had melted away.

There was a shuffle of feet somewhere before someone shouted, "Y'all get a room somewhere. Damn!"

Taariq smiled against her lips before pulling back. "Let's get you to your room."

"That sounds like a plan," she said, releasing her inner sex kitten.

He just smiled as he walked and supported her with his arm still wrapped around her waist. She did pretty well if you considered her inability to walk a straight line and she seemed to catch a serious case of the giggles halfway up to her dorm room. When she got her door open, Taariq took his cue to pull away. "Maybe I can call and check on you tomorrow?"

Anna's face twisted in disappointment. "You're leaving?"

"Yeah." He reached up and brushed a lock of hair away from her face. "I think you need to get a good night's sleep."

"Nooo." She tugged him into the small room by his shirt. "I want you to stay," she purred.

"Trust me. I'd love to stay. But I don't think that's really a good idea."

"Oh, really?" She kicked the door shut and started pulling up his shirt. "I thought that you wanted to see some of my other moves." Anna started swaying her hips. Once she got started, that shining glint returned to his dark gaze and she knew that she had him.

She kicked off one pump—maybe a little too hard because it flew high up in the air and smacked Taariq against his temple.

"Ow!"

"Oh." She slapped her hands across her mouth. "I'm so sorry."

Taariq rolled his eyes toward the door like he was reconsidering his exit.

Anna lowered her hands and doubled up on her awkward seduction show. However, this time she just leaned over to remove her other shoe. Problem with that though was that her balance was still a little off and so when she leaned… she kept on falling.

"Whoa! Watch it!" Taariq lunged forward, but unfortunately when she made a desperate grab for him, she just succeeded in pulling him down with her. She hit the floor and banged her head on the end of the nightstand.

"Anna?" he asked, concerned. "Are you all right?"

Again, Anna stirred and mumbled a string of apologies. She wasn't sure that they were getting through to him though. He looked a bit stunned and confused. "Oh. Are you all right?" She finally removed her hands and then tried to check to see if he was bleeding.

"Let me see."

Taariq pulled away. "I didn't hit my head. You did."

"Oh." She reached for her forehead but felt all right. "So where were we?"

"I was about to put you to bed. C'mon. Please."

She gave him her best puppy-dog eyes. "I'll be gentle."

He looked dubious at best. "I'm not quite sure that's at all possible with you."

She popped him on the shoulder. "Stop being a crybaby.

C'mere." Anna grabbed the sides of his face and jerked him toward her.

"I guess that means being gentle is off the table, huh?"

Anna smiled when she saw that there was no damage to his head. "You're fine. Here. I'll kiss it." She made a big production by making a loud smooching sound when she planted her lips to the side of his head.

Taariq chuckled and pulled away. His gaze met hers again and he couldn't help but smile again. "You're something else. You know that?"

She shrugged demurely and then became fascinated by his smile again.

"Let me guess. You want to kiss me again."

Anna sucked in her bottom lip and then nodded shyly.

Taariq laughed. "I swear I don't know whether to run or make love to you."

Finally, Anna's gaze roamed back to his eyes. "Well, let me help you out with that decision." She pulled his head back down and captured his lips in what could only be described as the most intoxicating kiss she had ever had in her life.

Granted she didn't really have a long list of those, but… damn. And when Taariq's hand started its slow climb up her leg, setting off another long trail of fire, she was lost.

Totally.

Completely.

It didn't really matter that they were tangled up on the floor instead of her bed. In fact, it kind of made it a little hotter. By the time her entire body was ablaze, she was impatient for Taariq to round toward second base. Kissing was fine—for good girls. But she was tired of being a good girl.

Grabbing the bull by the balls—well, not literally— Anna pulled at Taariq's shirt.

He broke the kiss. "Are you sure about this?"

Her answer was to yank the shirt over his head. After that, she pulled his face back so that she could continue to drink from his lips. With her eyes closed, she was able to enjoy the wonderful spinning inside of her head.

Taariq maneuvered their bodies around so that she could lay back flat against the floor while he took the dominate position. He broke their kiss and panted softly against the side of her neck while he tried to gain a little more control. However, when Anna started getting impatient again, she really went for it this time and shoved her hand in between his legs. When her hand gripped his bulging erection, her eyes fluttered open.

"Find anything you like?"

That can't be real.

"It's all me, baby." He winked and then stood up.

Speechless, Anna just watched as Taariq reached for the top button of his jeans and then slid the zipper down so slowly that he had her quivering with anticipation.

"You look like you're waiting to open a box on Christmas morning," he noted, sliding his pants down off his hips.

"I could make you a bow…but then you'd have too much on." She jiggled her brows. She liked this new saucy side. Maybe she should embrace it more often.

"You talk smack now. But I'm not so convinced that you can handle all of this, baby." His hands went to the waistband of his boxers.

"There's only one way to find out," Anna threw back at him.

He must have liked that answer because the boxers went sliding down.

Anna's mouth fell open as if her jaw suddenly weighed fifty pounds. Taariq hovered above her with his hands on his hips and his thick, long chocolaty erection sprung at least ten inches in front of him.

He laughed at her again. "What's the matter, cat got your tongue?"

"More like I've died and gone to heaven." She made a quick drool check and then grabbed his hand and pulled him down to her level. "I see what you're working with and I'm not scared."

"Good to know." He leaned close and peppered small kisses down the side of her neck. "Now it's my turn to see what you got." Reaching for the hem of her black dress, he waited only briefly to see if she'd back out. When no red light came on, he slid that baby up her firm legs, perfect thighs and her seductive hips. A smile hooked his lips when he saw her pretty pink Victoria's Secrets. "Nice," he whispered.

Still the dress went higher and revealed a flat stomach and an adorable outie belly button. By the time he reached her matching pink bra, he was practically salivating.

"Damn, Anna. Why do you always try to cover all this up? You're fine, girl."

She flushed. "You're just saying that because you're about to get laid."

"No. I'm saying that because it's the truth." He dropped his head and started nibbling just around the edges of her bra.

Anna moaned as if he'd entered her already and then proceeded to lose her mind when he managed to remove her bra like Houdini and suck her hard, puckered nipple into his mouth. Proving to be quite the multitasker, Taariq kneed her legs apart and settled himself between them.

The romantic in Anna had her lost in a world of fairy dust and unicorns. The way he was working her body had her feeling *that* damn good. And even when his hot mouth abandoned her caramel-dusted nipples to plant small kisses down the valley of her breasts, she was still moaning and squirming with total abandonment. Then his mouth settled around her belly button at the same time one of his long fingers dipped in between the small nest of curls in between her legs.

Wet. And growing wetter each second, Taariq quickly added a second finger and started massaging the base of her fat clit. Anna released a long "Ooooh" and then gracefully arched her back so that he could get in there deeper.

Amused by her greed, Taariq's laughter filled the small room. Even as he did so, Anna was more than aware of him inching farther down her body. At the first feel of his warm breath stirring the small hairs between her legs, her belly started quivering as if a swarm of butterflies were trying to find their way out. She expected Taariq to just plunge right in and make a feast of her, but once again, he surprised her by taking his time, sprinkling more kisses along her open thighs. Of course, that just drove her crazy, so much so that after a while, she reached down and tried to direct his head where she wanted it to go.

More laughter filled the room while Taariq stubbornly refused to relinquish his power. He knew what he was doing. He was a master at this. Anna had no choice but to endure the sweet torture of his slow thrusting fingers and the sensuous kisses he continued to plant all over her thighs.

Then there was this building pressure, rising in her fattening clit. A good sort of pressure that started to tingle deliciously. Her moans transformed into a husky whimper while her legs shook.

"Oh. I know what you're about to do," he said.

Anna tried to speak but suddenly English seemed too complicated.

Finally Taariq's head moved in the right direction and his two fingers glided out from underneath her clit to slide open her dewy lips. At the feel of his tongue slapping against her pulsing pearl, Anna came unglued and her orgasm detonated like a C-4 explosive. The air rushed out of her lungs, her eyes rolled to the back of her head and her entire body quivered and trembled with violent aftershocks.

And still, Taariq's tongue continued to twirl inside her like a Midwestern tornado. Before she knew it another orgasm was set to go off in 3…2…1…

"Aaaaah!" Anna's hips came off the floor and then she tried to wrench herself away from Taariq's merciless mouth.

He wasn't having it. When she moved, he moved. Before she knew it, she was gasping and crying when her third orgasm hit. Then…and only then, he let her go.

Taariq chuckled and gave her a full minute to catch her breath. "You all right?"

Embarrassed, Anna nodded but averted her gaze.

"Oh, don't get all shy on me now," Taariq said, grasping her left ankle and pulling her closer. "Show me that confident sexy kitten that was talking all that smack a few minutes ago."

Her embarrassment deepened, but somehow she managed to lift her head and smile.

"Ah. There she is." He leaned over and brushed a kiss against her temple. "All right, Ms. Thing. Now that you got me here, what are you going to do with me?"

Anna felt small next to Taariq's massive frame and for the first time she wondered, *what am I going to do with him?* In response, her gaze fell to his massive erection and another cycle of butterflies swarmed her insides.

"Give me your hand."

That command managed to pull her gaze back up to his smoldering eyes. Of course there was still amusement laced with raw lust dancing in his dark orbs.

"C'mon. Give it here." He held out his hand.

As if hypnotized, she followed his example and gave him her hand.

He smiled and leaned in for another kiss.

Anna met him halfway. She was already addicted to his taste. While their tongues danced with each other, Taariq wrapped her hand around his cock. It was hard, yet incredibly smooth. Curiosity led her to break the kiss so that she could stare down at the heady vision of his cock gliding smoothly in her hand.

"Mmm," Taariq moaned and then reached out for his pants where he retrieved a condom. He let Anna play for a little while, but then he quickly ripped open the foil and rolled the condom on in two seconds. "C'mere." He rolled Anna back down onto her back and once again took the top position.

Anna couldn't help but marvel at how slow and deliberate Taariq's lovemaking was…and that's exactly what it felt like—making love. Sure, she was just looking for a warm body tonight. She would've settled for a quickie. But this felt…intimate and special.

Was she crazy? Was she reading too much into it?

Both were a possibility. She closed her eyes and took another trip to the land of fairy dust and unicorns while Taariq performed magic all over her body. When he lifted her hips off the floor, she fluttered her eyes open so that their gazes could lock when he entered into her. Her mouth slowly sagged open as he eased what felt like unending inches through her tight walls. When it felt like he was nearing the center of her belly, she pressed her hands against his ripped abs and weakly tried to push him back.

"Almost, baby. Almost." Deeper and deeper he sank.

Restlessly, Anna tossed her head back and forth. She couldn't possibly take much more of him…and yet, she did. At long last, she could finally feel the base of his cock and the weight of his heavy balls sink against her opening. She whispered a gratitude that she had survived such an impalement and that he waited a few heartbeats for her body to adjust to his incredible size.

But then he started to move. His hips rocked slowly at first and then rotated in tiny circles.

Anna's mouth stretched wider, but she couldn't manage to emit a single sound. *Was he rammed against her vocal cords or something?*

"How do you like that, baby?" Taariq panted.

The cocky question was laced with amusement. He knew that he was rocking her world, turning it inside out. And when all she could manage was a whimpering moan, he elongated his strokes and stirred her honey pot so hard that she was slammed with two monstrous orgasms that had her clawing his back. When she finally managed to peek through the fan of eyelashes, she watched as ecstasy twisted his handsome features while a sheen of sweat blanketed his face. He looked like an African god, dominating her body as if it was nature's right to do so.

Their gazes connected and Taariq smiled wickedly before arching over and kissing her deeply. All the while, his hips never stopped. To no surprise, Anna's body started to quake again, but this time when she came, Taariq swallowed her whimpering moans.

How long they went at it, she didn't know. It seemed to go on for hours—but that couldn't be humanly possible. Was it? All she knew when she finally drifted off to la-la land was that their bodies were completely covered in sweat and she was completely satisfied.

It was just too bad that the next morning she woke up in bed alone and it would be over a decade before they spoke to each other again.

Fast Forward

Chapter 4

Today Anna was going to see him again.

For weeks she'd tried to prepare herself, but what she'd succeeded in doing was obsessing over what happened that night at the Kappa's frat party. She broke Stanley's heart, and Charlie and Taariq had broken hers. When she woke that next morning alone in her bed, without so much as a note saying goodbye or thanks for the hot sex, she felt like a two-dollar trick that'd gotten stiffed.

Not to mention the hangover. She must have spent two hours on her knees with her head hanging over the toilet and making all sorts of promises to God to get her through it. After that, she damn near scrubbed her skin off in a hot shower. If she remembered correctly Roxanne didn't come back to their dorm for damn near a week. By then, Anna had put in a transfer and ended up rooming with one of her closest friends to this day, Jade Stokes.

As for Taariq, he never tried to reach her and she certainly wasn't going to chase him. Clearly, he viewed that night as a one-night only situation and she was fine with that. Sort of. It was more like she just grew to accept it. Seeing how she'd stopped talking and tutoring Charlie, she'd stayed as far away from the Kappa Psi Kappas as she possibly could. That is until Charlie popped back into her life and fell in love with her baby sister, Gisella.

Initially she had mixed feelings about the whole thing since Charlie's ladies' man reputation had grown city-wide over the years. That is until he thought he was dying and actually went through his entire black book trying to make amends with all the broken hearts he'd caused, herself included. During that time, he and Gisella met. She'd moved from France after a big breakup herself. Either it was destiny or God simply had one hell of a sense of humor by bringing Charlie and Gisella together because today was their big day to enter into holy matrimony.

"Oh, God. I look huge!" Gisella despaired, looking down at her small pregnant belly.

"Don't be ridiculous," Anna chided, moving up behind her. "You're beautiful."

Gisella's gaze shifted to her sister in the mirror. "You really think so?"

"I know so." She winked and then gave her shoulders a quick hug. "Now let's get you married."

Gisella took a deep breath and then nodded. "I'm ready."

Anna wished that she could say the same. Any minute now, she was going to be face-to-face with Taariq Bryson and she still didn't have any idea what she was going to say if he spoke to her.

Ask him why he never called.

Anna quickly shook that suggestion out of her head. She didn't care why he never called, she told herself. If she said it enough times, she was bound to start believing it—despite that it had been more than a decade and it hadn't worked yet. Together, she and Gisella left the bridal suite and joined the other bridesmaids cluttered in the hallway. While everyone *oohed* and *aahed,* Anna's stomach started looping into large knots.

Any minute now.

She sucked in a deep breath as the group started toward the back lawn. As soon as Anna caught sight of a black tuxedo, she tensed. That is until she realized that it was just their father, Leonard Jacobs.

"There's my girls." His smile stretched as he opened his arms wide to envelop them both. "I've never seen a lovelier sight."

Anna and Gisella shared a proud look. It didn't matter that technically they were stepsisters. She from their father's first marriage and Gisella being from the woman he left her mother for. Somewhere along the way they'd agreed to leave the drama to the grown-ups and just cherish each other.

"Are you sure you want to do this?" he asked. "I have a getaway car souped-up with the valet."

Gisella laughed. "I'm sure, Daddy."

"Good. I think I like this joker." He tossed her a wink and then turned his eyes toward Anna. "You're next."

Anna immediately shook her head. "That's all right. I'm…good," she lied.

Her father frowned. "My little workaholic. I don't know what I'm going to do with you."

"There's nothing to be done. I'm happy. Really." It was clear from reading their expressions that neither one of them was buying into that malarkey.

"Let me tell you something, and I hope you listen to

your old man. Having a great job and making lots of money is great and all, but living and loving is the real key to happiness. Trust me on this."

Anna smiled through the awkward silence that trailed his words and almost sighed with relief when he returned his attention to Gisella. "So, let's get you married so that my grandson will be legit when he gets here." He offered his youngest daughter his arm.

Anna moved to stand behind Emmadonna so she could wait for the wedding planner to instruct them when to proceed. Then the music started up and Anna sucked in a deep breath. *It's time.*

A part of her wished that Taariq had just shown up for rehearsal last night so that she could have gotten this whole awkward moment over with. But since he had some business or something, he didn't make it. So now she just had to hope that she would be able to keep it together in front of two hundred people.

No problem. I can do this.

The wedding planner appeared and started directing the bridesmaids to start their procession. That was about the time when Anna's heart beat so loudly that it literally was drowning out the music. Finally it was her turn and she hesitated for just a beat before getting her feet to work. When she did, it just felt like two long rubber sticks that were about to drop her on her butt at any moment.

Then she saw him and oxygen fled her lungs as if they'd collapsed. Pristine in a sharp Armani, Taariq strolled like an experienced male model toward…Emmadonna. Smiling, he offered her his arm and then proceeded to waltz her down the aisle in front of Anna.

He didn't even look at me.

Insulted, Anna clenched her jaw and almost forgot to accept Derrick Knight's offered arm. He smiled. She didn't. Her gaze was too busy burning a hole in the back of Taariq's head.

Fine. If you're going to ignore me, then I'm going to ignore you, too.

She and Derrick parted ways so that they could take their positions on opposite sides of the reverend just as the wedding march began to play.

An hour later, Gisella and Charlie Masters's hands overlapped as they gripped the knife and together sliced into a Sinful Chocolate popular creation: white chocolate and lemon cake. The happy couple smiled at the wedding photographer and then toward each other before shoving a handful of the decadent dessert into each other's faces.

Laughter rippled among the large gathering of friends and family and then a cheer went up when Charlie tried to kiss and lick his wife's face clean.

"I love you, baby," he whispered, snapping their bodies together despite the small baby bump and dipping his head for a long soulful kiss. She tasted so sweet.

"J'taime, aussi," she responded when he allowed her to come up for air.

Charlie groaned at the instant hard-on he acquired whenever Gisella spoke French. Now that they'd said their "I do's," Charlie was ready to skip right to the honeymoon phase. So much so he found himself asking Gisella every five minutes, "Can we leave now?"

"Behave." She giggled and then allowed Anna to pull her away.

"I'm so happy for you, Gisella," Anna said, wrapping her arms around her baby sister. "I don't think the Lonely Hearts will ever admit it, but you've renewed our faith in love."

Gisella smiled and wiped away a stray tear from her

sister's face. "I owe you so much. If you hadn't gone to see Charlie that night…"

Anna gave Gisella's waist a gentle squeeze. "I'm sure you would've done the same for me."

"In a heartbeat." She paused. "He's out there, you know. There's a perfect guy out there for you."

Anna shrugged. "Maybe. But until then, me and Sasha are going to be just fine."

Gisella smiled as her eyes spied on Taariq as he walked across the lawn.

Anna followed her gaze and then experienced another punch in the gut. The sight of him just laughing and having a good time churned her stomach. "You know, I'm going to run to the ladies' room. I'll catch up with you later."

"Oh. Okay."

Charlie was laughing while his mother gripped his cheeks and tried to pinch the blood out of them. "My baby has made me so proud! Not only did you give me a beautiful daughter-in-law, but I'm finally getting my *grandbaby*."

Taariq turned just as Gisella's sister strolled away from the bride and groom. *I swear that girl looks familiar.* He studied her long-legged stroll, soft round curves and searched like hell through his memory for an answer, but he kept drawing a blank. Finally he gave up and strolled over to the newlyweds.

"Mama Arlene," Taariq greeted, coming up behind Charlie's mother. "I don't know if Charlie told you, but we talked it over and he's completely cool with calling me Daddy. All you have to do now is accept my proposal. I'll make an honest woman out of you," he flirted.

"You're so bad." Arlene blushed as she gave him a welcoming hug. "Now when are *you* getting married?"

"As soon as you say yes," he dodged. *Marriage is not for me.*

She rolled her eyes. "You just love me for my fried chicken."

"That's not true. You make a mean sweet potato pie, too."

Arlene laughed and giggled like a schoolgirl when Taariq asked, "Would you like to dance?"

Mama Arlene clapped her hands together. "Oh. I'd love to."

"Then I'm your man." He winked and then offered her his arm. As he led her to the pavilion before the band, Charlie was left to shake his head.

"So you finally did it," Hylan said, stepping forward and slapping his large hand across Charlie's back. "You waved the white flag and surrendered to the enemy."

Charlie laughed and rolled his eyes. "Don't start that with me."

"What?" He hunched his shoulders. "I'm just saying. We were supposed to be playas for life. Remember?"

Derrick rushed up behind Hylan and quickly put him into a headlock. "Whatever he's saying, don't listen to him."

"Oh, he's harmless." Charlie chuckled. "I'm just waiting for the day when he starts waving his own white flag."

"It'll never happen," Hylan croaked from under Derrick's arm and tried to tap out.

"It doesn't make any sense to be so hardheaded," Derrick said, releasing him.

Hylan sucked in a deep breath and then playfully sent a left jab against Derrick's shoulder. "Mark my words. A brother like me ain't going down without a fight. You'll have to pry my playa's card out of my cold dead hands."

"All right," Derrick said. "We're going to hold you to that."

"Charlie," Stanley said, joining the group. "Your wife's cake is off the hook. What's her secret, man?"

"She didn't make this cake. Her assistant Pamela insisted on making the cake as a gift. She did a good job."

"Pamela, huh? Where is she?" Stanley turned to survey the crowd. "Maybe I'll marry her."

"I'm sure she'll be thrilled to hear it." Charlie laughed. "Start with baby steps. Try to get a date first."

"Or try to get a woman to stand still long enough for you introduce yourself," Hylan added, laughing. It was a tradition to give the lanky redhead a hard time.

"Ha. Ha. Ya'll gonna get enough messing with me." Stanley scanned the crowd again. "There's gotta be someone here I can hook up with. Weddings are the best places for single people to hook up. That and funerals."

Hylan and Charlie just stared at him.

"What? It's what I heard."

"We're going to pray for you," Hylan said, rolling his eyes. How his white brother managed to hang with them for fifteen years and still be as square as he was was nothing short of amazing.

"Whatever." Stanley moved his lanky frame closer to Charlie. "So now that you're off the market what do you say to passing a playa like me your infamous little black book? I've heard that it's pretty thick."

"A playa like you?" Hylan snickered. "If anyone should inherit the Holy Grail from my man here, it should be me."

"Guys, guys. As much as I'd like to improve your game, I can't. Gisella and I had a nice farewell ceremony and then tossed the book into the fireplace."

Hylan and Stanley blinked and then both pointed at him accusingly. "Judas!"

Derrick and Charlie laughed.

"What do a couple of married women have to do to get a dance with their husbands?"

Derrick and Charlie turned toward their smiling wives.

"Not a thing," Charlie said, taking his wife into his arms. "Of course, I'm looking forward to a little private dancing," he whispered as he led her toward the music.

"Oh, you'll get your dance, Mr. Masters. That and a whole lot more."

"That's what I'm counting on, Mrs. Masters. That's what I'm counting on."

At the open bar, Anna ordered a gin and tonic. She didn't normally drink, but today she fully intended to celebrate love winning out for a change. "Thank you," she said, accepting her glass and then drifting toward the dance floor. From there, she watched as couples spun around the dance floor. But none were more beautiful than Charlie and Gisella. It was heartwarming to see how they smiled and gazed into each other's eyes. It was as if no one else existed at this fairytale delight. It was just the two of them swaying in perfect time to "At Last."

"One day," Anna whispered with blossoming hope. But hadn't she been saying that to herself for a while now? She sucked in a deep breath and tried to block out all the reasons it wasn't her out there on that dance floor being spun around in a strong man's arms.

So where is my perfect man?

Anna tilted up her glass just as Taariq twirled Arlene Masters around the floor in front of her. The sight was unexpected and she nearly spit out her drink. She tried to hold on to her anger, but she couldn't help looking him up and down. *Damn. He's gotten better looking since college.* She wasn't sure how that was even possible. Her gaze continued roaming over his six-foot-four physique, especially those wide, mountainous shoulders, trim waist and impressively firm backside. Her mouth went dry even though she was still sipping on a drink.

"Fine, ain't he?"

Anna jumped. "Huh? What?" She glanced down and saw that she'd spilled her drink. "Damn."

Emmadonna snickered while she patted the top of her dress dry. "I know what you're thinking and I think you should put it right out of your head. Just because one of those Kappa boys is getting married, it doesn't mean the rest of them are marriage material." She turned up her cocktail.

"I wasn't thinking anything," Anna lied. If she was proud of anything it was that she had never told any of her girlfriends about her and Taariq. That would have been a nightmare.

"Uh-huh. So you were drooling like a starving dog staring at a milk bone just for the hell of it?"

"No, I wasn't," Anna said, averting her gaze as if that would stop the rush of heat blazing through her body. "I was just…just…"

"Yeah. Save it." Emmadonna laughed.

Anna rolled her eyes. She hated how her best friend could read her like a book. Despite being annoyed, her gaze drifted back to the dance floor. At that moment, Taariq glanced up and the corner of his lips lifted.

"Humph!" Emmadonna settled a hand on her thick hip. "It's been a while, but I definitely know *that* look."

Somehow Anna managed to shake off the strange spell that had come over her. "What look?"

"Oh. Now you're going to play crazy?"

"One of us is crazy—and I guarantee you it's not me." She gave Emmadonna a hard look and then walked past her. "Excuse me."

Stunned, Emmadonna watched her waltz away. "Now that's a damn shame. No wonder that child hasn't been laid in so long. She can't see when a man wants to jump her bones." She tsk'ed and shook her head. "Damn shame."

The song ended and Taariq politely bowed to Arlene

Masters while pressing a kiss to the back of her hand. "Thank you for the pleasure."

Arlene giggled like a school girl. "You're such a player," she said cheekily.

"Guilty." Taariq laughed and then winked. "But let's just keep that between us."

The next song began to play and an older gentleman appeared at their side. "Mind if I cut in?"

"Not at all," Arlene answered, slipping her hand from Taariq's and offering it to her new partner.

Taariq arched his eyebrows in amusement. "Looks like the kettle was calling the pot black, Ms. Player."

"I'll keep your secret if you'll keep mine."

To that, Taariq threw his head back and laughed. Once he strolled off the dance floor, he scanned the crowd for Gisella's sister. He wanted to get to the bottom of this mystery. But after searching around and coming up empty, he decided just to shrug it off.

Spotting his boys, he made his way over to where they were just hanging out. "Looks like another one bites the dust, fellahs. I still can't believe it." He swung his gaze over to Hylan. "I gotta tell ya. I thought you'd fall before old Charlie."

Hylan choked on the rest of his champagne. "Who? Me?"

Once Hylan finally managed to suck enough air into his lungs, he waved Taariq off. "How the hell can you say something like that? It's like you're calling me out of my Christian name or something."

"All right. Don't be overly dramatic," Taariq said, shrugging. "It's just that…you know…you and Shonda hooked up again."

"And? Just because I'm seeing some chick I used to date a while back you think that's just cause for me to jump off a cliff?"

"I've just never known you to recycle."

Hylan cut his gaze toward Stanley.

"Me, either," Stanley said.

"*And* you brought her to the wedding," Taariq added.

"So? It's just a pit stop. We're flying out to Saint Lucia this afternoon for a little sun and fun. I haven't had a vacation in I don't know how long—and I need one."

Taariq laughed and snapped his fingers in front of Hylan's face. "C'mon, man. This is basic Playa Handbook 101 stuff here. You never bring a chick to a wedding unless you plan on marrying her. You bring a chick here and they get to seeing a wedding dress and all these pretty little flowers and the next thing you know they're plotting on how they're going to get *you* down the aisle."

Hylan bobbed his head.

Shonda threaded her way through the crowd. The young, budding actress drew her fair share of stares, but it probably had more to do with the fact she was practically wearing a hooker's uniform—an extremely short silk minidress that left nothing to the imagination.

The men in attendance seemed to like it.

The women…not so much.

Hylan glanced at his watch. "It's about that time. I'm outta here." He turned and gave both Stanley and Taariq half hugs and fists bumps.

"What? You're not going to wait for the garter toss?" Taariq teased.

"Get the hell out of here with that mess, man." Hylan laughed and then strolled across the pavilion to retrieve his date.

Taariq shook his head. "Damn shame. If he doesn't watch it, he's going to mess around and end up married."

"Who? Hylan?" Stanley asked. "Please. It'll never happen."

Taariq thought about it for a moment. "Yeah. Maybe

you're right." He glanced around. "I need a drink. I'ma head up to the bar. Do you want something?"

Stanley held up his own drink. "Nah. I'm good."

"Cool. I'll be back." Taariq made his way over to one of the bars when he found just the woman he'd been searching for. Straightening the sleeves of his tux, he moved in right for the kill with his game face on.

"Bartender, a brandy," he ordered from behind her and eased to her side so that he could lean against the counter. "A nice day for a wedding," he casually commented.

Ms. Tall, Brown and Beautiful cut her brown eyes toward him, which melted the smile right off his face. "I'm sorry, miss. I didn't mean to bother you."

"Miss?" She finally turned toward him, but her features refused to soften. For about ten seconds she just glared at him. "You don't even remember me, do you?"

Damn it. I knew she looked familiar. Problem was that he still couldn't come up with a name. Embarrassed, Taariq tried to cover by laughing.

She steadfastly refused to be amused.

The bartender set his brandy down in front of him.

Taariq quickly tossed it back in order to give his brain a little more time to get him out of this jam. Problem was that it didn't work.

"I'm waiting."

"You're, um, Gisella's sister," he answered, knowing damn well that wasn't about to fly with this lady. Luckily there was a divine intervention.

"Anna! Is that you?" Stanley said, cutting toward them. "It is you! I don't believe it." Stanley thrust himself in between them and pulled *Anna* into a tight embrace. "You know I kept staring at you during the ceremony, wondering if it was you and it is!"

"Stanley, it's so nice to see you again," she said.

Taariq stood on the sidelines while her name looped in

a vicious circle inside his head. There was a small thread of something that lay just beyond his recollection.

"You know you broke my heart back in the day," Stanley confessed. "I had a mad crush on you then."

"I'm sorry," she said with genuine affection.

"It's okay. You let me down easy. One of the few who did." Stanley laughed. "Wow. So you're Gisella's…?"

"Older sister," she supplied, smiling.

"Huh. Small world," Stanley marveled, staring at her like a lovestruck puppy.

That didn't alarm Taariq too much. Stanley got that look a lot when it came to women.

"Well, I better get going," Anna said, reaching for her drink.

"Oh, you don't have to go, do you?" Stanley asked. "I was hoping to convince you to go out to dinner some time."

"Oh…well, uh…"

"C'mon. I promise I'm not the same goofy guy I was back in college."

Taariq clamped his mouth shut on that one. The last thing he wanted to do was throw shade on Stanley's handicapped mack game.

Anna looked as if she was falling for his man's puppy dog expression.

"All right." She reached for the small purse dangling off her arm and then handed over a business card. "Give me a call."

Stanley lit up. "Will do."

Taariq slowly realized that he'd just been outplayed by none other than Stanley. He glanced around casually to make sure that there were no witnesses to this.

"I'll talk to you later," Anna said and then turned and stepped on Taariq's foot.

"Damn, baby. Watch where you're wielding…" His gaze

shot up when his brain finally booted. "Wait a minute." He snapped his fingers. "I remember you now!"

"Oh, good. Now I'll have some satisfaction when I do this!" She tossed the drink dead in his face. "Enjoy the rest of your day," she said sweetly and then strolled off.

Chapter 5

The next Saturday, Taariq strolled through the doors of Herman's Barber shop with a big grin on his face when he saw the usual suspects were already there. "Yo, wassup?"

"Hey, Big Man," they shouted back at him.

Herman's was the place to be to discuss women, politics and sports. The perfect place for men to just be themselves, to get and give advice and just plain bond with one another. Men in the neighborhood filtered in and out daily, but Saturday had always been Herman's busiest day of the week. Six barbers ranging from old school to new school donned burgundy barber jackets with Herman's name scrawled across the back. For an old redbrick building, the shop still managed to look modern and brand-new.

Herman Keillor, a tall robust man who was cruising toward his mid-seventies had owned the busy shop for over forty years. Most of the guys filtered through to hear Herman's stories, tough-love advice and get sharp haircuts.

Taariq came for the stories and the haircuts. It's not that he had anything against love, he didn't. Especially now since he'd seen how happy Derrick and Charlie were these days. He just didn't think it was for him. The whole settling down thing with one woman for the rest of his life was just too foreign. He was like his father that way.

Growing up with just his dad, he liked to think that he'd learned all he needed to know about women—how to catch them, how to reel them in and, more important, how to let them go. He was never cruel or anything like that. Honesty was always the best policy. Unfortunately, when you told women that you were not looking to settle down, ten times out of ten that just challenged them to try and change your mind. It was odd. Women always claimed that men never talked, when the truth was more like they never listened.

"So what are we going to do with you today?" Herman asked after Taariq settled his large frame into his chair.

"Just edge me up, old man."

Herman snapped out the cape and then wrapped it around Taariq's neck. "All right now. I done told you about all that *old man* mess."

Taariq laughed and then turned his gaze toward the mounted flat screen that stayed religiously on ESPN. "How are our Braves doing?"

"They're still looking pretty good," Herman said, turning on his razor.

The bell over the door rang and Bobby, Herman's college-aged grandson and J.T., the local street hustler, strolled through the door at the same time.

"You're late, Bobby," Herman chastised, while giving Bobby a stern look over his wire-rimmed glass.

"Sorry about that, Grandpa. I guess my alarm is broken."

"It'd work if you set it."

"Point taken."

J.T., of course, made a beeline straight to Taariq. "Yo, T. My main man. How's it hanging? You know I got some great merchandise for you today."

"Man, I ain't looking to buy nothing today."

"Yo, that don't mean that you can't do a little window shopping. NawhatImean?" He jerked open his coat, which he'd been wearing in eighty-degree weather, and flashed Taariq with his latest inventory of gold and silver chains.

"I'm going to have to pass, man."

"You sure, man? You being my man and all, I can offer you a good discount."

Taariq laughed. "I'm sure."

The bell above the door jingled and Derrick and Stanley strolled into the shop. A round of greetings ensued as they made their way over to the barber chairs.

"Hey, T, man. Whassup?" Derrick exchanged dabs with him.

"Nothing much. I'm just getting this noggin' cleaned up for the ladies. You know how I do." He turned his fist toward Stanley and waited for his dab, but his brother left him hanging. "Oh, it's like that now?"

Stanley shrugged his shoulders. "Do you remember what you did to Anna?"

Taariq lowered his hand as he huffed out a long breath. "Man, I told you. I didn't do nothing to your girl. The girl is crazy."

"Women don't just throw drinks in people's faces for no reason," Stanley countered.

"Right. Hence why I called her crazy."

Herman turned off his clipper. "You want to be still or you want to walk around town with your head looking jacked up."

Taariq huffed at the rebuke, but kept still.

"That's what I thought." Herman turned the clippers back on.

Stanley continued to stare Taariq down, weighing whether or not he should believe him.

Taariq was offended. "C'mon, man. Have I ever lied to you?"

At last Stanley relaxed. "I'm not accusing you of lying. I just find the whole thing strange. That's all."

"You and me both. But I'm not going to sweat it or anything. It is what it is." He said it so smooth that he almost believed it himself. Truth was ever since she tossed that drink in his face, he'd been racking his brain about what he could've possibly done to deserve to be embarrassed like that.

"Well, I guess it doesn't matter, since I'm the one that scored a date with her." Stanley puffed out his chest. "Clearly she's into me."

"The other white meat," Derrick said and cracked up all of those who were listening.

"Ha. Ha. Chuckle it up," Stanley told him. "All of y'all are a bunch of haters anyway."

"Hardly," Taariq barked. "You average about one real date a year, not counting those pity booty-calls with that chick down at the Waffle House, and we're supposed to be hating on you? Brother, please."

More laughter.

Stanley brushed his shoulders. "Whatever, dog. Say what makes you feel better because I saw how you were peeping ole girl out before I swooped in and got the digits."

Herman shut off his clippers again. "Wait. Let me get this straight. Breadstick over there stole a girl out from under you?"

Every head in the place swung from SportsCenter over to Taariq. Surely they all thought that their ears were playing tricks on them.

Taariq felt the heat. His reputation was about to take a monstrous hit. "C'mon now. Y'all ain't going to believe that, are you?" He tried to laugh, but it was clearly forced and awkward.

"Well, I never thought I'd see the day," Herman said and then swung his gaze back over to Stanley. "Looks like your haircut is on the house today, Stanley."

The fact that the old man called him by his real name and not by one of his many monikers wasn't lost on the crowd and a raucous cheer sounded off.

Taariq's ego was a little bruised, but seeing Stanley getting mad respect from all the brothers in the barber shop made him feel good for his Kappa brother. "So when is this little date happening?"

In between the many congratulatory pats on the back, Stanley shrugged. "Probably sometime this week. Her schedule is a little crazy, but it's definitely on."

Taariq started to bob his head when he received another warning from Herman.

"Be still or I'm going to have to shave it all off."

"All right, old man. Chill." He looked back over to a grinning Stanley. "So where are you taking Anna?"

"I'm thinking about taking her over to the Atria in Buckhead."

Bobby whistled. "That place is nice."

"I figured some low lighting, soft music, good food and then she won't be able to turn down these baby blues." Stanley tossed Taariq a wink.

"Well, I hope y'all have a good time." He grinned back and tried to ignore the hard kick in his gut.

Chapter 6

"I've decided to become a lesbian," Emmadonna announced at the beginning of the Lonely Hearts Club's monthly book club meeting. Currently, it was a book club that never really got around to reading or discussing any books. It had long transformed into a two-hour gossiping session between old college-girlfriends that leaned heavily on the male-bashing side.

A collective gasp rose from the other three members, while their eyes bulged.

Anna's mug slipped in her hand, splashing hot coffee into her lap. *"Damn it!"* She jumped to her feet, sat the mug down and then proceeded to vigorously wipe the coffee from her lap while a scroll of profanity rolled off her lips.

"Glad to see that you guys are taking it so well." Emmadonna snickered.

"Are you joking?" Jade asked and then quickly turned to Ivy. "She has to be joking, right?"

The petite and usually soft-spoken Ivy boomed, *"She better be!"*

"Wait. Wait." Emmadonna held up her hands. "Hear me out."

Anna ignored the need to race back to her bedroom to change out of her comfortable sweatpants to do just that. "This better be good."

"Well, when you think about it, it makes logical sense. How long have I been coming to these meetings bitching about how hard it is to find a good man—five years? Hell, I'm not getting any younger and nowadays we have to fight off the whole rainbow nation chasing after straight men with just as much vigor as the women. Single black women are getting killed out here."

"So your solution is to become gay yourself?" Anna asked for clarity.

Emmadonna's big shoulders shrugged. "If you can't beat them, join them."

The women chuckled and shook their heads at what they clearly perceived as a joke.

Jade rolled her eyes as she brushed her auburn, curly locks back from her shoulder. "You're either attracted to women or you're not. You don't just wake up one morning and decide to become gay."

Emmadonna waved off what was clearly common sense and crossed her thick legs. "I don't see why not. Besides, I hear that doing it with a chick is so much better anyway. We know what gets us off—mentally and physically."

"I'm not having this conversation with you," Anna said, finally making her exit from her living room to go change her pants. She didn't believe that Emmadonna was going to swing to the other side of the fence any more than she believed Idris Elba was going to knock on her door and propose with a long-stemmed rose clenched between his teeth.

"Y'all will come around. Watch," Emmadonna shouted behind her.

Anna rolled her eyes one more time and then slammed her bedroom door behind her. Sure, it was a hell of a landmine out there in the dating world, but batting for the other team was going a bit too far. She didn't have a problem with gay people, but for her she was strictly dick-ly, despite the multi-year dry spell she was on. Nowadays she tried to convince herself that she really didn't mind the fact that she hadn't been in a serious relationship for a while. After all, she had dated her fair share of thieves, liars and cheaters—actually, a little more than her share. As a result, she'd decided to take a little break—the operative word being *little*. Turned out that once she jumped out of the dating pool, she got used to not swimming with sharks or playas as they liked to call themselves. It had been rather nice not always having to dissect and discern what men said versus what they truly meant anymore. Things like "No. I'm not seeing anybody" usually meant, "What my girl don't know won't hurt her," or "Sorry I didn't call you back, I've been having problems with my phone" meant, "I was out screwing around with another girl."

Maybe Shakespeare had it right. All the world is just a stage and everyone's an actor—in a very bad play. Searching for something real was like trying to find a needle in a haystack. She hated to admit that she had given up, but in reality she had. If a man smiled at her, she would give him her best *get lost* stare. If a brother got past that and tried to talk to her, she'd give simple one-word answers in a monotone voice. If he asked her for her number, she'd ask him point-blank—*why?* The one thing she wouldn't do was get her hopes up.

Hope was for teenage girls.

Disappointment was for those same girls twenty years later.

"Anna, are you coming back out here or what?" Emmadonna's bullhorn voice easily penetrated her bedroom door.

"Coming!" Anna quickly changed out of her gray sweatpants into her navy sweatpants. Hey, it was her normal weekend attire and when something works, you stick with it. "All right. Where were we?" she asked, rushing back out to her circle of friends.

"We've been out here listening to Emmadonna's crazy B.S. while you were hiding in the bedroom."

"It's not B.S.," Emmadonna countered while jabbing a balled-up fist against her thick waist. Despite looking like an angry Amazon woman, the rest of the group still refused to take her seriously.

"Does anyone want more coffee?" Anna asked, grabbing her mug.

"I'm good," Jade answered.

Everyone else shook their heads.

"Sooo," Emmadonna shouted toward the kitchen. "When are you going to tell us what that whole thing between you and Taariq Bryson was about?"

Anna almost dropped the coffeepot. "What?"

"Don't play crazy. You left that man standing there, looking like a fool. What did he do?"

Acted like he didn't remember screwing my brains out and then dumping me back in college. "Oh. It was nothing." She finished pouring her coffee and then went back to join her friends.

They all stared at her with their arms folded.

"What?"

"Surely you don't think any of us is buying that story," Jade said.

"Just drop it. I don't want to talk about it," she said curtly.

The girls all looked at each other and then tossed up their hands.

"All righty then." Ivy cleared her throat. "I have an update on that Jamaican brother that I finally went out with last week if anybody wants to hear about it."

A fresh dating story grabbed everyone's attention.

"You mean that Mandingo god that was grinding up all on you at Gisella's wedding a few months back?"

Ivy bobbed her head while her usually pretty caramel complexion darkened a deep burgundy. Everyone picked up on the telltale sign at the same time.

"Ooooooooh!" they chorused, scooting up in their seats and leaning toward Ivy as if that would ensure they would hear the dirt faster.

"I thought your ass was walking funny when you rolled up in here this morning." Jade snickered.

"I did, too," Anna admitted, dropping back into the chair closest to Ivy. "C'mon. C'mon. Don't leave us hanging. Did you sleep with him?"

"Wait. Don't you want to hear about where he took me for dinner?"

"No!"

Emmadonna clarified. "All I want to hear is, how big is he? How long did he go? And how many orgasms did you have?"

"Then you can tell us about dinner," Anna added as if that would make their inquiry seem less crass.

"And which was better, the food or the sex?" Jade added. "I say the sex because I came a few times just watching him work those hips on the dance floor."

Emmadonna's head swiveled in Jade's direction. "You, too?"

"Hey!" Anna waved a finger at them. "Don't be rude.

You two could be talking about Ivy's new man. Besides, I thought you were gay now, Em?"

"Oh, yeah." Emmadonna frowned. "This may take a little more time getting used to."

They rolled their eyes and shook their heads in sync before returning their attention to Ivy who was steadily turning beet-red.

"First of all, I didn't intend to sleep with him."

"Of course not," Jade said, placing a hand on Ivy's knee for reassurance. "You're a good girl."

"Yeah," Anna cosigned. "None of us even remembers those ménages à trois you used to participate in back in college."

"Or the swingers' club you and your ex used to frequent a few years back," Jade added.

Anna held up a finger. "And don't forget when you used to juggle those three boyfriends back in the '90s."

"Yeah. Weren't they cousins or something?" Emmadonna asked.

"I think so." Anna struggled to remember.

Jade turned back to Ivy with a deadpan expression and said, "We take it back. You are a slut."

"It's always the quiet ones," Emmadonna added.

Ivy's jaw dropped open, but instead of protesting she cracked up. Once she started, they joined in.

"Y'all ain't nothing but a bunch of jealous heifers," Ivy said.

"Jealous?" Jade countered. "How do you figure?"

"Because I'm the only one in the group that has gotten laid since Obama got in office."

Their laughter quickly dried up with Jade mumbling under her breath, "Oh, no, this heifer didn't."

Ivy tried, but couldn't stop laughing since she had successfully delivered a zinger that shut them all down.

Her getting the best of the loud group was a rarity, and clearly she was going to milk it.

"Fine, bitch. Keep your damn stories to yourself," Emmadonna finally countered while she wiped the invisible mud off her face.

"C'mon." Ivy jumped out of her chair to go hop into Emmadonna's lap and wrap her arm around her wide shoulders. "You know I love you, girl."

"Better not sit in her lap long," Anna said. "She might start feeling you up."

Ivy popped up like a toasted Pop-Tart and rushed back to her seat. The women howled, especially Emmadonna.

Anna just barely made out a knock on the front door. "Hold that story, Ivy." She jumped up and rushed to answer it. Just because she wasn't having sex, didn't mean that she couldn't live vicariously through her friends…or friend, since Ivy so rudely pointed out that she was the only one nowadays getting some action. Had she really not had sex since the Bush years?

With her mind still calculating the hard math, she opened the front door. Then that whole sex thing was wiped clean from her head when a very pregnant Gisella beamed a smile at her from the other side of the door.

She squealed in delight as she flung open her arms. "Oh, my God. What are you doing here?"

Gisella waddled her way into her sister's arms and asked in her thick French accent. "What? I have to have a reason to come and visit my own sister?"

"Of course not," Anna said, giving her a good hug. "You know that you're welcome here anytime." Then she added in a lower voice. "You know what day it is, right?"

Gisella pulled her sister's arms. "Oh. Are the girls all here?"

"Is that Gisella I hear at the door?" Emmadonna's booming voice asked from the living room.

"Does that answer your question?" Anna said.

Gisella just smiled and then proceeded toward the sound of laughing women. The moment she entered the living room, there were squeals of delight before they rushed to pull her and her *very* pregnant belly into warm hugs.

"Oh, my God. You look like you're getting ready to drop that load at any second," Jade marveled.

"She better not. I just had this carpet cleaned," Anna joked.

The women laughed, but waved off the concern.

"You're definitely having a boy. I can tell by the way you're carrying."

"Doctor says I'm having a girl," Gisella informed them.

"Oh, please. What the hell do they know?" Emmadonna said, rubbing Gisella's belly.

"And how many babies have you had?" Anna asked, shaking her head. Let Emmadonna tell it, she was an expert on everything…except on how to keep a man.

"Okay. Believe fat meat ain't greasy if you want. I call them like I see them and I haven't been wrong yet."

"Fat meat ain't what?" Gisella asked, twisting her face. "I don't think I know this American expression."

"It's a Southern thing," Ivy reassured her. "It just means you can choose not to believe the obvious."

"Oh," Gisella said while the other women laughed at her bewilderment. "Well, I don't care what I'm having as long as it has ten fingers and ten toes…and will stop laying on my bladder like it's a La-Z-Boy."

The women shared another laugh and then took turns trying to feel the baby kick. When Anna placed her hand against her sister's belly and felt her little niece or nephew deliver a karate chop against her hand, she was surprised by the rush of tears.

"Are you all right?" Gisella asked her softly.

"Yeah." Anna quickly swiped at her eyes. "It's just amazing that…there's really a little baby in there."

Without missing a beat, Emmadonna quipped, "Oh, lawd. Anna has forgotten how babies are made."

"I didn't say that." She popped Em on her shoulder. "I know how babies are made. I just find that the whole process is this fantastic miracle." Anna glanced up into her sister's eyes. "And I think that you're going to make a wonderful mother."

Gisella's eyes misted with tears before the sisters were hugging again.

Anna put on a smile, but she would be lying if she said that she didn't feel something else tugging at her heart. Something that she really didn't want to put a name to, but no matter how hard she tried to ignore it, she knew exactly what it was: envy. How was it that she, someone who had been in the dating game a few years before her baby sister, was still single with no prospects on the horizon? Gisella had been in Atlanta less than a year and had snapped up a good one and now had a baby on the way.

Then again that's probably what she got for tossing in the dating towel.

"So what's going on, ladies?" Gisella asked as she eased down into a vacant chair. "What man are we castrating this week?"

Anna winced. "Please. It's not like that," she said as a weak defense to their monthly male bashing.

"Actually," Jade said, plopping down next to Gisella. "So far, Emmadonna's announced her bid to become America's Next Top Lesbian and Ivy was just about to give us the 411 on that fine Jamaican she picked up at your wedding."

Gisella frowned.

"You know," Jade pressed. "The one that was doing all that bumping and grinding with her on the dance floor."

Emmadonna clapped her hands together and then started

snapping her fingers and crooning, "I don't see nothing wrong…with a little bump and grind, baby." What made her performance hilarious was her attempt to bust out the old "Tootsie Roll" moves with her legs and hips.

"Oh. You mean Reece?"

"Oh, is that his name?" Em cracked up. "We've been calling him Mandingo."

Ivy rolled her eyes. "I've been trying to tell them that I actually had a nice time with Reece the other night. He was a complete gentleman."

"Oh, no. You didn't roll up in here to spit none of that gentleman crap. We know the brother got the panties," Em sassed. "The question on the table is whether *Reece* can lay the pipe like his hips promised he could?"

Despite it being a crass question, all eyes zoomed toward Ivy, anxious for her answer.

"His pipe-laying skills were…on point."

The room erupted with squeals and laughter.

"I knew it! I knew it!" Jade jumped up and performed a dance like a running back after a touchdown. "Did he have to peel you off the ceiling? How close did you get to Jesus?"

"Mighty close," Ivy confessed. "He was sweating. I was sweating. The silk sheets were sticking to every part of our bodies and when he busted out the strawberries and chocolate syrup, I was in hog heaven."

"Well, alrighty then. That's what I'm talking about." Emmadonna held up her hands and received a series of high fives. "At least someone is getting some for the team."

"Says the woman that just switched teams," Anna chirped.

"What?" Gisella asked.

Anna shook her head. "Never mind. You don't want to know. Besides you don't have to worry about dealing with singlehood anymore. You got yourself a good man."

"You could have yourself a good man, too, if you would just put yourself out there more. Give up *CSI: Miami* and *Snapped* nights."

"Oooh, girl. *Snapped* is my show," Jade interrupted while reaching for her coffee. "Did you see the one when homegirl superglued her man's dick underneath his balls? That heifer wasn't playing."

The circle of girlfriends bobbed their heads.

"That was actually a repeat," Anna said. "I think that is going to go down as a classic."

Gisella shook her head. "Do you girls hear your-selves?"

"What?" Emmadonna jabbed a hand against her hips. "It's a crime to watch television now?"

"It's not that you watch it, it's *what* you watch. It's all these negative images and messages about men, women and relationships. It's effecting your vibes—your auras. People can pick up on these things—men especially."

Em waved her off. "Oh, please."

"I'm serious," Gisella insisted. "You get what you put out there. Now I'm not saying that you won't run into a couple of dogs out there, but if you step out there expecting them *all* to be dogs, then it's like blowing a dog whistle." Gisella turned toward her sister. "You know what? I'm going to find you a man." She slapped her sister on the knee.

"What?"

"You heard me. Just leave it all up to me."

"What about the rest of us?" Jade said.

Gisella laughed. "I love you girls, but only God performs miracles."

Chapter 7

Two months later...

"Yo, Taariq!" the entire crowd in Herman's Barbershop greeted him the moment he walked through the door.

"Mornin'." He gave everyone a short salute.

"You're late," said Herman Keillor, peeking over his wire-rimmed glasses.

Taariq glanced at his watch and saw that he was indeed five minutes late. "Sorry about that, old man. I'll do better next time." He winked.

"Make sure that you do. You know I don't like any of that CP-time nonsense. Come on over," Herman directed. "I got your seat all warmed and ready."

Taariq strolled over and plopped into the leather chair.

"So what's been happening?" Herman asked, smiling and draping a black cape around his neck.

"Just been chillin', I guess."

"Well, that's good. Don't want to overdo it."

J.T. pimp walked his way in the door and made a beeline over to Taariq. "T, my main man. You know I got you today, baby."

"Oh, really? What you got?"

"Looky here. I know you're a ladies' man, so I got you the latest Beyonce *and* Alicia Keys." He reached into his magic jacket and produced two CDs. "Bam! Whatcha think about those?"

Taariq shook his head. "Nah, these two ladies are a bit too young for me."

"Too young? Man, you trippin'." J.T. stuffed the CDs back into his pocket.

"Nah." He glanced around. "Ayo, where's Bobby?"

"Lord knows," Herman said, shaking his head. "His ass is late, too."

"Hey, didn't school just start? Maybe you should cut the college kid a break."

"I'm cutting him a check for that damn tuition. The least he could do is show up for work on time."

Sensing he'd wandered into sensitive territory with Herman's grandson, Taariq tossed up his hands. "Sorry 'bout that. I didn't mean no harm. I was just trying to stick up for a fellow Kappa man. You understand."

"Uh-huh." Herman clicked on his clippers.

The shop's bell jiggled again, but this time it was Derrick and Charlie strolling through like regular rock stars. They were greeted with a round of the perfunctory, "Yo, whassup?"

"Hey, what's happening, captain?" Taariq asked, grinning.

"You got it," Charlie said.

His boys made it over to his chair and exchanged a couple of fist bumps.

J.T. popped his head back up. "What about some DVDs?"

"Will you get out of here with that," Charlie said, laughing. "You know we never buy none of that bootleg crap. Why do you keep asking?"

"Closed mouth don't get fed," J.T reasoned.

Derrick shrugged. "The man makes sense."

The door jiggled again and a smiling Stanley strolled inside. "Yo, everybody, whassup?" he said in his best Vanilla Ice impersonation. Everyone was used to the white man who thought he was black and just hollered back at him.

"Looks like we're all here," Taariq said.

Derrick frowned. "You mean Hylan is still not back yet?"

The Kappas shook their head.

"Hell, has he even bothered to check in?" he asked. "It's not like him to be gone this long."

"He left me a message a couple of days ago," Taariq remembered and pulled out his cell phone. "I haven't had a chance to call him back."

"Get that man on the phone," Charlie said. "At least so that we know his ass is still breathing."

Taariq held up a hand. "Herman, could you hold on a second?"

Herman cut off his clippers. "Sure. I live to wait on you guys," he joked.

Taariq found Hylan's home number in his cell's contacts and hit the call button. A second later the line was ringing. Then a woman answered the phone. "Hello, is Hylan there?"

"No. I'm sorry he's not. This is his sister-in-law, Barbara. Can I take a message?"

Taariq pulled the phone away from his ear for a moment and stared at it.

"What's wrong?" the Kappa boys asked in unison.

"Um, yeah," Taariq said, putting the phone back to his ear. "Just tell him that Taariq called."

"Oh, would you like to talk to his wife?"

"Uh, no. That, um, won't be necessary. I'll just get in touch with him later." He disconnected the call.

"What was that all about?" Stanley asked.

Taariq looked up. "Guys, how do y'all feel about making a trip out to the Caribbean to meet Hylan's *wife?*"

Saint Lucia

On the beautiful island of Saint Lucia, Taariq stood fiddling with his tie while Hylan gave him and the other Kappa brothers the 411 on how he met his wife—well, his soon-to-be wife—Nicole Jamison. Every other sentence was cut off by him or one of the other Kappa brothers asking Hylan to run something by them again. Unbelievably, this Nicole had moved into Hylan's vacation home nearly two years ago and told everyone in the Soufriére quarter that she was Hylan's wife, which wasn't true. Everyone bought her act because Hylan rarely came to the island. Not only that, somehow, someway she managed to get everyone to fall in love with her. It was a pretty good scheme, of course, until Hylan actually showed up.

What Taariq couldn't wrap his brain around was why Hylan didn't just put her on blast and call the cops. Sure, he supposed that Nikki was a good-looking woman. She even seemed nice, too. But she had to have made one hell of a batch of Kool-Aid to pull off a stunt like this. Given the beaming smile on Hylan's face, he must've drank a few gallons of it, too.

"You mean to tell me that she was up here frontin'?" Taariq said after finally picking his jaw up off the floor. "Who the hell does that?"

Hylan's smile stretched wider. "I know it all sounds a little odd. But—"

"A little odd?" he thundered. "Try crazy as hell."

Another one of his fraternity brothers, Derrick Knight, drew a deep breath and settled a hand on Taariq's shoulder. "Calm down."

"Calm down? Are you for real?" Taariq said. "Our man has either got caught slippin' or has lost his mind. Either way, it ain't good."

Charlie, Derrick's best friend, shook his head. "I don't know. He looks pretty sane to me. He's just in love."

"Figures. Your mind ain't been right since you met Gisella." Taariq huffed out a long breath and rolled his eyes.

Derrick opened his mouth.

"And don't you say nothing because you're the one that set off this whole domino effect." Taariq started to look misty-eyed. "How could you guys do this to a brother?" He shook his head and started pounding his chest. "I thought we were boys. We were supposed to ride this bachelorhood thang until the wheels came off. Playas for life. Remember that? Now look at y'all. Make me the last brother standing and everything."

Stanley stepped forward. "Hey, man. You're not alone out here. You know you always got me."

Taariq pursed his lips together and gave the other brothers a look that said, *"See what y'all done left me with?"*

Hylan laughed. "Look, man, I know what you're saying. I was talking that same crap just a few months ago."

"Ah, yeah." Charlie bobbed his head. "Guess you waved that white flag of surrender, too, Mr. It's-Never-Gonna-Happen."

Hylan tossed up his hands. "All right. All right. I deserved that one." He chuckled at all that mess he was talkin' at Charlie's wedding. "Just charge it all to the game, I guess, because I'm marrying Nikki *today*."

Taariq shook his head and mumbled, "It just ain't right."

Derrick glanced over at Charlie. "You know Isabella and Gisella are going to be mad that they missed out on a Caribbean wedding."

Charlie shook his head. "True. But Gisella is too far along in her pregnancy to fly anyway. At least that's the excuse I'm gonna lay on her."

"Humph. Well, I'm going to direct all Isabella's complaints straight to the man who's responsible for this sudden rush," Derrick said.

"Send her my way," Hylan said. "I got this."

Knock. Knock.

"Come in," Hylan yelled.

Momma Mahina, Hylan's estate caretaker pushed open the door and stuck her head inside. "The reverend is here. Think you guys can be ready in five minutes?"

"I'm ready now." Hylan puffed out his chest.

His boys laughed at his eagerness.

"Damn, man." Taariq slapped a hand against Hylan's back. "My bad. You really are sprung." He struggled to wrap his brain around that.

Smiling, Hylan shrugged his friend's hand off his back. "All right. Keep poppin' that B.S. That just tells me that your ass is gonna be next."

Taariq's hands shot up in the air. "Now don't try puttin' no hexes on a brotha. I ain't puffing on whatever it is y'all puffing on."

"Then I'll be next," Stanley declared.

All eyes turned toward him.

"Are you even seeing anybody?" Derrick asked.

"Bump that. When was the last time you had a date?" Charlie razzed.

Stanley puffed out his thin chest and waved his brothers off. "C'mon now. Y'all know I gets the ladies."

They all gave him the "get real" stare.

"A'ight. A'ight," Stanley said, determined not to pay them no mind. "Watch, I'm gonna find me a honey so fly, y'all gonna be trippin' over your tongues."

Derrick winced. "Honey?"

"Fly?" Charlie asked.

"See, that's your problem right there," Taariq said. "You're still stuck in the '90s. Just be happy that Tawanda over at the Waffle House takes pity on you and breaks you off a piece every once in a while." *Stick with her and leave Anna alone.*

The brothers cracked up laughing.

"All right. We better get ready to do this." Hylan said and then remembered something. "By the way, I got this business venture I want y'all to all to take a look at soon."

They all looked at him with the seemingly sudden change of topic.

"My baby girl wrote this cool play and I want you guys to consider investing in it."

Once again, the men exchanged looks. "All right, man," Derrick said, holding up his fist and giving his man dabs. "You got it."

Hylan beamed as each one cosigned on the deal.

Two minutes later, Hylan and the Kappa Psi Kappa brothers pushed and squeezed their way through the two-story palatial villa. The moment the people realized the groom was coming through, a sudden cheer went up and people finally started moving out of the way.

"Damn. Is everybody in the Caribbean in here?" Taariq grumbled. It was strange to see such a herd of people crammed into the house. One would think that they were attending some celebrity wedding.

"Trust me. They're here for my wife." Hylan chuckled. "They're crazy about her."

And it was true because the little whoop that Hylan had created was nothing compared to the full-out cheer that went up when Nikki and her small entourage made their way down before the smiling reverend.

"I guess you weren't kidding," Taariq whispered. Again, he noted that the bride to be was indeed a beautiful woman, but he couldn't help the knot of distrust hardening in his stomach. Could it be that his buddy Hylan got snared by a gold digger? He wouldn't be the first brother to fall victim. He had to hand it to this Nikki chick, she was creative.

Taariq glanced back over at Hylan. The brother was so far gone, it was sad to watch. Big moon-eyes, goofy-ass smile, Taariq suspected that all this Nikki chick had to do was say jump and Hylan wouldn't even ask how high. He would just start bouncing his butt all up and down Saint Lucia like a wild rabbit. Restraining from shaking his head, he somehow managed to carve on a fake smile and stand in as the best man while hating every minute of it.

When Nikki finally stopped to stand by Hylan's side and Reverend Oxford launched into his ceremony, Taariq started to mourn the carefree playa lifestyle that he and his Kappa brothers used to enjoy together. One by one, their small dog pack was collapsing. No more competing for the finest women at the club. No more bragging about who lassoed the wildest freak. Hell, for that matter, no more late nights of any kind. Any day now, Charlie's wife was about to push out their first rug rat and Derrick and Isabella were actively trying to get pregnant.

How in the hell did all of this happen so fast?

Taariq's gaze roamed to his left toward a grinning Stanley. A chuckle bubbled up in his chest. He loved Stanley like a blood brother, but Doogie Howser had more game than the over-eager redhead. If he was reduced to having Stanley as his sole wingman, he was going to have to take the brother under his wing and upgrade his playa status.

"I do," Nikki said smiling and jarring Taariq out of his private reverie.

A beat later, it was Hylan's turn. "I do."

It was all Taariq could do not to groan out loud.

"With the power invested in me, I now pronounce you husband and wife." Reverend Oxford slapped his Bible closed. "You may now kiss the bride."

Hylan sealed the fiasco with a kiss.

The house roared with applause and a second later the bride and groom were literally bum-rushed for handshakes, hugs and kisses. After seeing her sister being jerked from one embrace to another, Barbara Jamison panicked and took on the role of bodyguard.

"Careful, careful. The woman is pregnant!"

A hush fell over the crowd as Barbara gasped and then slapped both hands over her mouth.

Nikki timidly hunched her shoulders up. "Surprise, honey."

Charlie reached over and waved his hand before his friend's eyes to make sure that he was still with them. "I think you're supposed to say something," he whispered.

Hylan pumped his fists straight into the air. "Yeah, baby! Victory!" He rushed over and swooped his wife into his arms and spun her around.

Nikki squealed with delight before Hylan smothered her with kisses.

Taariq glared and then shook his head. Another Kappa brother down.

Chapter 8

"If you're going to be my number one wingman then you're going to have to start looking the part," Taariq informed Stanley as they headed toward the weight room at Gold's Gym. "First things first, we're going to have to start putting some real muscles on that scrawny little frame of yours. I can't have you messing up my A-game with the ladies."

"Yo, man. You don't have to worry about that," Stanley said, puffing up his chest. "You *know* I gets mine. When we roll up in the club we're going to be like the perfect one-two punch. You know what I mean?"

Taariq would have laughed if it wasn't for the fact that Stanley was being dead serious. Instead, Taariq cracked a patient smile and swung his arm around his new best buddy's pencil-thin neck. "Look, my man, having confidence is one thing—being delusional is another."

Charlie, who was marching two paces behind them, cracked up.

Stanley tried to turn around, but Taariq held him firm. "Don't pay him no mind. Charlie's macking days are behind him. All he has to look forward to are sleepless nights and Diaper Genies."

"And don't forget a beautiful wife to spoon at night and wake up next to every morning," Charlie interrupted, clearly unfazed by his Kappa brother's endless teasing.

"Spoon?" Taariq asked, stopping dead in his tracks. "Damn, brotha. You're already whipped that bad? Only women want to spoon. Men *fork*. You feel me?"

"Yeah," Stanley agreed, bobbing his head. "Men fork."

Taariq and Charlie's gaze cut over toward Stanley who looked like a Howdie-Doody bobblehead.

Stanley's smile cut in half. "What? I'm just saying."

Charlie cracked up. "You got your work cut out for you, man. Good luck."

Taariq couldn't agree more, but he'd always enjoyed a good challenge. "Chuckle it up," he said. "When I get through with Stanley, he's going to have so many ladies giving up the panties he'll have a permanent hump and lockjaw."

Frowning, Stanley pressed a hand against the side of his jaw. "Really? Why?"

Taariq and Charlie stood staring at Stanley like a couple of deer caught in headlights. When it was clear that their buddy was serious, Taariq felt his first stab of doubt about turning Stanley into a good club wingman. All the real playas know that they are only as good as their wingman since women travel in packs. A good wingman distracts and flirts with the rejected women while the playa makes a move on his target dime piece. If all goes right, the playa scores the digits or is able to pry his target away from the pack for some one-on-one time either on the dance floor or in a corner booth.

However, if the wingman steps to the pack with a weak game, they'll chew him up and then spit him out. No way are they going to let their girl give up the real digits, let alone allow one of their own to escape to the dance floor. They'll just circle around and start talking so much trash, both playa and wingman would be lucky to limp away from the table with their pride and ego shredded to hell and back.

Taariq wasn't going out like that. From this day forward, Stanley was in some serious training, like Rocky before going after the big Russian dude.

"Don't worry," Stanley said, his chest swelling with confidence again. "Just think of me as your blank canvas. I'm here to learn from the master."

Taariq shook off that one stab of doubt and then thrust up his thumb. "Now that's what I'm talking about. Total commitment to the cause. You see this, Charlie?"

"I see it. I'm just choosing not to believe it." He trucked on toward the weight room.

"What? You're doubting my skills?" Taariq asked, following.

Charlie kept shaking his head. "My name is Les. I ain't in that mess."

"Yeah. All right, Mr. Married Man. Trust and believe that you're going to miss club-hopping with your boys. That one-man-one-chick thing is just too old-school." They pushed open the weight room door and made a beeline straight toward their regular bench press. "Now, don't get me wrong. With you three stooges out of the picture that just means more ladies for me."

"Us," Stanley corrected, thumbing his chest. "More ladies for *us*. I'm the wingman, right?"

Taariq's smile turned plastic. "Right. That's what I meant. *Us*."

Still snickering, Charlie started adding weights to the

weight bar. Clearly he didn't see the point of hiding his doubts about Taariq's makeover plan. After all, hadn't they all tried at one time or another? Stanley was who he was, a nice, smart guy who was loyal to his friends. He was also goofy and awkward when it came to anything dealing with grace and movement, and he didn't have an athletic gene in his entire body.

"All right. You'll see," Taariq stressed, having nowhere else to go with his argument. He tossed his black bag down near Charlie's.

"If you say so." Charlie squatted down onto the bench and started strapping on his gloves.

Taariq restrained the impulse to ask Charlie whether he'd like to put his money where his doubt was, mainly because that one sliver of doubt he felt ten minutes ago was already starting to widen and expand. How did one go about establishing a playa boot camp? He snuck a side-glance at Stanley who was busy stripping out of his wife-beater and revealing a thin and pasty white chest that could probably heal the blind if he was standing in direct sunlight.

"Damn, Stan. Haven't you at least attempted a push-up in your entire life?" Taariq asked, reaching over to see whether there was any muscle definition in his biceps.

"Sure." He hedged a bit. "Well, not the full-on army-type push-ups."

Taariq frowned. "Then what kind do you do?"

"The half ones." At Taariq's confused look, Stanley went on to explain. "You know. The ones where you bend your knees and you spread your hands out farther apart."

Taariq's heart dropped like a stone. "You mean *girl* push-ups?"

Charlie slapped his knee and rocked his head back with a hearty laugh while Taariq weighed the option of working the clubs as a solo pickup artist.

A red wave of embarrassment crept up Stanley's face. "Well, I don't think that it's fair to call them *girl* push-ups. It's harder to do than it looks."

"I'm sure it is," Charlie said, lying back and positioning his hands on the bar. "T, get over here and spot me."

Petulant, Taariq folded his arms. "Let Stanley do it. He needs to get the practice in."

Charlie's eyes doubled in size. "Say what?"

"Really? Can I?"

Taariq gave Stanley a sly grin as he slapped him on the back. "Of course you can. There's nothing to it. You just stand over here behind Charlie's big football head while he pushes out about four sets of twelve. Any time you see that he needs a little help pushing the bar up, you just reach down for the bar and help him lift it back onto the weight stand. Simple. I'm sure that you've seen us all do this a million times."

"Yeah. But no one ever said that *I* could spot for them."

"Well, I certainly don't want to be the one to break that record," Charlie said.

Taariq waved off Charlie's concern. "Don't mind him. He's just acting like a punk. You can do this."

However, Charlie wasn't having any of this crap. He hopped up off the bench so fast, Taariq and Stanley half-way expected to discover a spring in the center of the bench. "You know what? If you're serious about this makeover, maybe Stanley should go first."

"All right. I'm down." Stanley jumped to take Charlie's place.

"Chicken," Taariq mumbled under his breath.

"No. I don't have a death wish. I have a baby on the way, remember?"

Stanley clapped his hands and then rubbed them together. "Okay. Let's do this." He reached for the bar and both Taariq and Charlie nearly had a heart attack.

"Whoa! Wait!"

But Stanley was way ahead of them and foolishly lifted the weight bar off its cradle and just as quickly, it was coming back down toward his head.

Both Charlie and Taariq grabbed the bar and lifted it back up. Once Taariq placed the bar back onto the stand, he barked, "Man, don't you *ever* do that again. What are you trying to do, kill yourself?"

Stanley sat up, shaking and clutching at his throat. "I think I just saw my entire life flash before my eyes," he gasped.

"Was it just as sad and disappointing the second time around?" Derrick asked, strolling into the weight room and catching the tail end of the conversation.

"Yo, man. You're late." Taariq walked over to his buddy, slapped hands together and shared a shoulder-bump.

"What? Are you the truancy officer now?" Derrick frowned and shook his head.

"Nah, man. I'm just saying." Taariq shuffled around and tried to appear nonchalant, but the fact of the matter was that he was having a hard time getting used to all the changes that were happening with his boys. It wasn't just the fact that he was reduced to transforming Stanley into his wingman. It was the number of cancelled basketball games piling up, *Monday Night Football* games interrupted with wives buzzing about everything from decorating to showing off their latest baby sonogram images—in the middle of the game. And his boys were cool with it!

Everything was changing.

Taariq hated change.

"Don't sweat it, man," Derrick said, shrugging and setting down his bag. "Isabella and I had a doctor's appointment this morning."

Taariq's heart stopped.

"And?" Charlie asked with a twinkle in his eyes and a growing smile.

Derrick's smile stretched and looked about as goofy as Charlie's. "And...*we're* pregnant!"

"Ahh, man. Congratulations." Charlie launched toward Derrick and locked him into a bear hug.

Stanley jumped up and got into the mix as well, slapping Derrick's back as his own form of congratulations. "Big D, man. I know that you're going to make a cool father."

"I certainly hope so," Derrick said. "Right now it just seems so surreal to think I got a little seed growing. You know what I mean?"

"I know *exactly* what you mean." Charlie laughed. "These past eight months I've been on one long emotional roller-coaster ride. Frankly, there's nothing out here that really gets a man prepared for the big changes, especially the ones that are going on with my wife. In the past week alone I've run out more times in the middle of the night for these weird cravings. Last night it was Krystal burgers and pistachio ice cream."

The brothers frowned.

"I know. But how about I ate half of it? And it wasn't *that* bad."

Taariq withheld his congratulations and just shook his head. "I don't even know what to say to all that."

Derrick snickered. "Oh, you'll find out one of these days, T. Don't think you're going to be able to hold out on that walk down the aisle much longer. Trust me. Your days are numbered."

Taariq waved him off like he was a gnat bothering him. "You don't know what the hell you're talking about, D. When I said that I was a playa for life, I meant that. Just because my three supposed best friends punked out doesn't mean that I'm about to."

"Oh. Is that how you see us?" Derrick asked, laughing. "We're all a bunch of punks?"

Taariq shrugged like he was just calling it like he saw it.

"All right. All right." Charlie tossed up his hands. "I'm going to let you have that because clearly you're still tripping."

Taariq laughed. "If you say so. C'mon, Stanley." He patted his buddy on the back. "Let's get you started on something a little simpler—like the dumbbells."

Stanley's eager face collapsed into disappointment. "B-but…I thought I was going to learn—"

Taariq swung an arm around Stanley's neck, choking off the rest of his sentence. "Don't sweat it, man. We all have to crawl before we can walk and we got to break you in with the basics before you hurt yourself. You feel me?"

Stanley nodded, but a frown still hung on his face.

"Trust me on this. When I get through with you, you're going to be ready for the cover of *GQ* magazine."

"Really?" His smile returned while his eyes started to twinkle as if he was trying to picture himself on the cover.

"C'mon, man. Would I ever steer you wrong?"

Charlie and Derrick opened their mouths, but Taariq quickly shot them a deadly stare that successfully shut them up. Well, almost. They did snicker a bit.

Taariq allowed them to get it out of their systems. It didn't matter. He was going to give Stanley the makeover of his life. Before he directed his protégé toward the other end of the weight room, Derrick pressed a hand against Taariq's shoulder and stopped him.

"Are you forgetting something?"

There was a second where Taariq wondered what his buddy was talking about before he remembered. "Congratulations on the kid. You and Isabella are going to make great parents."

Derrick's brow quirked up. "You mean that?"

"Partially. I think Isabella is going to make a great mother. You—I'll be praying for."

They all barked with laughter and then went about getting their morning workout in. Mentally, Taariq still struggled with the changing dynamics between him and his friends. But the truth of the matter was that Taariq was never big on change, despite it being something that happened all the time. Being the only child and raised by a single father, he grew up constantly moving from one city to another, never staying long enough to develop any relationships—male or female.

So when he finally enrolled in college and joined the Kappa Psi Kappa fraternity, it was the first time in his life he felt like he'd actually found or belonged to a real family. The Kappas were his brothers, through and through. There was nothing that he wouldn't do for them and vice versa. Well, at least he hoped that was still true.

Taariq pushed his thoughts to the back of his mind and tried to concentrate on the sweaty mess that was Stanley. The man was a waterfall just after the warm-up.

"How is it that you've been coming to the gym with us every morning for the past fifteen years and you have *no* muscle definition?"

Stanley grabbed his towel and mopped his forehead. "Well, actually, I just, um, come to shoot the breeze. Keep up with the 411. You know." He gave Taariq a sheepish grin. "But don't worry. I'm committed to the grind. Just think of me as a blank slate. Do with me as you wish." His words drifted across the weight room, causing Charlie and Derrick to start snickering.

Taariq twisted his face.

"Okay. That didn't come out right," Stanley said.

"You think?" Taariq drew a deep breath. "Just keep you and your blank slate far away from me and we'll get along just fine."

There was more laughter from the two peanut-heads across the room, but Taariq ignored them and proceeded to put Stanley through a modest workout to see what he was working with. Answer: not much.

Sweat continued to pour off Stanley just curling twenty-pound dumbbells. When it came to doing leg squats, Taariq had never seen so much shaking and trembling going on. He kept checking around to make sure that they weren't in the middle of an earthquake. But it turned out that nothing else was shaking—just Stanley's bony legs.

"This is going to take longer than I thought," Taariq mumbled under his breath. One thing was for sure, he wasn't going to toss in the towel. He loved a challenge.

An hour later, the four grabbed their bags and headed back to the showers and then left the gym. Derrick and Charlie headed out to the airport. Charlie was flying Derrick to Washington for some political event. A sore Stanley walked out to the parking lot like he had a stick rammed up his butt.

"I don't think I'm going into the office," Stanley moaned, heading toward his car. "I need a nap."

Taariq slapped a hand across Stanley's back and encouraged him. "Toughen up because this is just the beginning." He tossed him a wink and then headed over to his baby: a brand-new, week-old, black Mercedes-Benz. Walking toward the driver's side, he stopped briefly to check out his reflection in the shine on the hood. After giving himself a wink, he quickly jumped behind the wheel and peeled out of the parking lot. Ten minutes later, he was stuck in Atlanta's morning traffic and cursing himself for not leaving the gym sooner.

As usual his mind started wandering while he inched

along downtown. But before he could get into anything too deep, Stevie Wonders's "Isn't She Lovely?" started playing somewhere in the car. Confused, Taariq started looking around. When he discovered it was coming out of his gym bag, he crammed his hand inside and pulled out an iPhone.

Taariq didn't own an iPhone.

On the screen, it read *My Boo.* "Hello?"

"Ch-Charlie?"

Taariq frowned. "Uh, no." He glanced at the phone again and then down at the bag. "Damn. I think I grabbed the wrong bag at the gym."

"Hoo—hoo. It's time."

"Time? Time for what?" he asked, though he suspected that he already had an answer.

"The baaaabyyyy," she screeched and then returned to that weird breathing. "Hoo…hoo…hoo…hee…hee… hee."

"What are you doing?"

"Bre-breathing. Where's Charlie? I need him to come home."

"Uhhh…"

"Hoo…hoo…hee…hee. Tell him to hurry."

Taariq started twisting around in his seat. Cars started blaring their horns. "Charlie…is…um, he's not here. I—"

"I—I need him. I—I have to get to the hospital."

"But—"

"NOW!"

"All right. Um, I'm on my way."

Chapter 9

It was 9:00 a.m. and Anna was already on her third cup of coffee. She had been up all night reviewing proposals from K & L Corporation, a large conglomerate that had an interest in acquiring her company, Odyssey. Since the downturn in the economy they had been able to fend off a lot of corporate raiders, but the president of her company had been talking more and more about retiring and he hadn't been so quick to turn down buyout offers.

In some ways, the president's change in position felt like a knife being jammed in the center of the back and at other times there was this huge, strange…sense of relief. Maybe this was just the type of change she needed in her life. Heaven knew that she needed something to get her out of her rut. She just didn't know what it was.

Riiiinnng.

Anna frowned while she wiggled her feet into her pumps. Since she was cutting it close on time, she decided to let the call go to voice mail while she tried to hightail it toward the front door.

When her high heel nailed Sasha's fluffy orange tail, she meowed and then swiped her thin nails across Anna's right ankle. "Oww!" Anna hopped up and Sasha took off like an orange bat out of hell, screeching the whole way. "Sorry!" she yelled after her pet, but clearly her tabby didn't want to hear it.

Anna took one step and winced at the sudden stinging pain in her ankle. When she glanced down, she saw that it was bleeding through four jagged clawed lines. "Great. Just great."

Riiiinnng.

Anna rolled her eyes. "All right. All right. I'm coming." She hopped on her good leg over to the phone before the call was transferred to voice mail. "Hello."

"It's time!"

"Excuse me?" She wasn't sure that she caught the voice.

"The baby," Gisella screeched and then went into this weird hyperventilating breathing thing. "It's…it's coming."

"Oh! The baby!" Gisella's words finally registered. "You're in labor?"

"Y-yes!"

"Great. Okay." Anna's heart leaped as she lowered her foot. "All right. I'll just meet you and Charlie at the hospital. I can't believe it. I'm about to be an aunt!" Giddy, she started to hang up the phone when Gisella screamed over the line.

"Wait!"

Anna pressed the phone back against her ear. "What is it? Is something wrong?"

"Ch-Charlie is out of town. Hoo. Hoo. Heee. Heee. I need

you to come and…take me to the hospital. I mean—Hoo. Hoo. Heee. Heee—if it's not too much trouble."

"Oh. Um. All right." Now her heart was doing some wild African beat. She halfway expected it to pound its way out of her chest at any moment. Despite her nerves, she wasn't about to let her sister down. "Sure. I can do that. I, um…"

"Now. Come now."

"Gotcha. I'm on my way." She dropped the phone back onto its base and started running around, completely forgetting about her battle scar from Sasha. "My purse. My purse." She ran around in a circle and then finally grabbed it and bolted toward the door. However, the moment she jerked it open, she remembered that she needed something else. "My car keys. My car keys." She raced around in another circle until she found her keys on the hook by the door—just where they were supposed to be.

"Calm down. Pull it together," Anna mumbled repeatedly. But she was having a hard time getting her body to listen to reason and her thoughts to stop chasing each other. She was not a woman accustomed to falling apart so she sent a quick prayer up that she wouldn't start doing so today.

When she reached her car in the parking deck of her high-rise condominium, she experienced another mini-heart attack when her car wouldn't turn over. "No! Oh, God. Not now. Please!" Anna turned the key again and for half a second her silver Lexus LX flirted with the idea of starting, but then changed its mind at the last second.

"Damn it!" She smacked the steering wheel and then jumped when the horn blared. Now with her heart in the center of her throat and her stomach churning, Anna sucked in a deep breath. "C'mon, baby. Please. Please, don't do this to me now." She turned the key again. There was a slight hesitation, but this time, at the last second, the engine roared to life. "Oh, thank you, baby!" She planted a kiss against the steering wheel and then quickly peeled out of the parking garage.

However, her mad dash ended the moment she hit the congested street outside her condominium. "What the hell?" Anna looked up and tried to see if she could make out why traffic was so bad, but it all looked like one giant parking lot. "I don't believe this."

On cue, Anna's cell phone started ringing from her purse. Without missing a beat, she fished through the cluttered bag, pulled out her iPhone and read her sister's name. She answered with a preemptive, "I'm on my way."

"Hoo. Hee. How far are you?"

Hearing the stress in her sister's voice, Anna laid on her car horn. "Um. Not too far. I guess I should be there in a few minutes." *I hope.*

"Good. Okay. Hurry."

Anna disconnected the call and released a long stream of curses before laying into her horn again. *"Move! Damn it!"*

If none of the hundreds of drivers that Taariq was pissing off in Atlanta's downtown traffic didn't kill him, then surely the police would pop up at any minute and haul his butt off to jail. He cut people off, tailgated, laid into his horn and rolled down his window to give drivers who were just creeping along a good tongue-lashing. In between driving like a maniac and having temporary Tourette Syndrome, Taariq tried to get Charlie on his phone. Each time, Taariq was transferred to his own voice mail.

"Oooh. You're going to owe me big time for this one, buddy," he hissed and then tossed the phone back into the gym bag.

Ten minutes later, he pulled up into Charlie and Gisella's suburban home, thankful that he'd made it without a scratch on his new Benz. He jumped out of the car and drew in a deep breath. *You can do this.* Another deep breath and he rushed toward the door.

Taariq knocked and then rang the doorbell. When no one came to the door, he tried again. He glanced around to check that he was at the right house. Had Gisella found another ride? Called an ambulance?

A rush of relief flooded him at the thought. There was no need for him to play Superman and try to save the day. Besides, he didn't know nothing about birthing no babies.

Right then, he should have turned around, got in his car and drove off. Instead, he tested the door. Even then, it wasn't too late to execute his escape plan. But noooo. He pushed open the door and entered a scene that was going to forever change his life.

"Hoo. Hee. Hoo. Hee."

Taariq cocked his head. "Hello? Gisella? Are you in here?"

"Hoo. Hee."

Maybe—just maybe—he still could've run out of there with his tail tucked in between his legs, but he continued easing into the house like a curious cat. "Gisella?"

"Hoo. Hee. I'm in here," she called out weakly. "Hoo. Hee."

This definitely didn't sound too good. Taariq's stomach looped into tight knots while his heart hammered so hard his rib cage ached. However, it wasn't in his nature to just punk out. He was a man, after all. He could handle anything tossed his way. All he had to do was get a pregnant woman to the hospital. How hard could that be?

Now that he was finished with his mini-pep talk, he forced a little more steel into his spine and quickened his step. Yet, the moment he walked into the large, open living room and spotted Gisella trying to sit or squat, he wasn't sure which, another wave of panic washed over him and that little bit of steel he'd injected melted like lead. He knew without a doubt that this was going to be harder than he thought.

A lot harder.

"Hoo. Hee." Gisella tried to squat lower to the ground. Her face was twisted with pain and her long hair was drenched with sweat and matted to the side of her face.

For a few seconds, Taariq stared openmouthed, while waiting for his brain to kick into gear. That was just about the time Gisella abandoned her practiced *Hoo-Hees* for a very high-pitched shriek that exploded Taariq's panic button.

Eyes wide, Taariq raced over to her. "It's okay. It's okay. I'm here." He took hold of one of her arms. "Let's get you to the hospital."

Gisella took hold of his right hand and crushed it. "Arrrrrrghhhhh!"

Shocked by her seemingly superhuman strength, Taariq's mouth sagged as he tried to pry his hand free. Unfortunately, the more he struggled, the tighter her grip became. At one point, he even thought he heard his bones crack.

"Gisella, breathe," he urged. "Please, breathe."

To her credit, she tried. Gisella took a quick sip of air, but in the next nanosecond she was back to blasting a hole in his eardrum and breaking the rest of the bones in his hand. "Arrrrrghhhh! Where's Charlie?"

"I don't know. I don't know. I swear I don't know."

Mercifully, whatever pain that had her in its throes suddenly released her and she loosened her iron grasp on his hands.

"Oh, thank you, sweet baby Jesus," he panted, snatching his hand away. He lifted his hand up to his face and saw that it looked permanently disfigured.

"H-hospital," Gisella panted as she pulled herself up from her deep squat. "Get me to the hospital."

Taariq tried to stretch the muscles in his fingers, but it wasn't working. He opened his mouth to complain, but Gisella popped him on the back of his head.

"Now!"

Taariq dropped his hand and jumped to attention. "Right. Okay. Um, let's go." Despite the pain in his hand, he tried to escort her to the door. For his troubles, she shoved him away and gestured toward a suitcase sitting next to the plush sofa. "Get my bag."

"Right. I'm on it." *Hurry up before her head starts spinning.* He raced over to the bag, grabbed it with his good hand and started for the door.

"Arrrrgggh!" Gisella started squatting again.

Taariq dropped the suitcase and rushed back over to her. "No. No. No squatting. Let's get you out to the car."

"I…can't," she screamed through clenched teeth. She tried to grab his hand again, but he snatched it out of her reach. "The baby is coming. I can feel it."

"I know. That's why we have to get you to the hospital," he said gently, trying to pull her out of her squat. "Now if I can just get you out to the car." He turned up a tight smile, but received a scold for his trouble.

"Don't you think I'm trying to get to the car?" she snapped with her nostrils flaring. "Hell, I wouldn't be in this position if it wasn't for *your boy, your homie!*"

"Ooookay." Taariq couldn't believe that the usually sweet and kind Gisella was quickly turning into a fire-breathing man-hater right before his eyes. "I'm sure Charlie would be here if he could or if he even knew what was going down right now."

"Hoo. Hee. I should've known that you would take his side," she growled with her eyes narrowing. At this moment, it wouldn't surprise him if her head started spinning. "You

Kappa men just stick together, don't you? Through thick and thin."

Taariq opened his mouth to respond, but at the last second thought better of it. There was a real possibility that he could end up saying the wrong thing and wouldn't live to tell the tale.

"Uh-huh. That's just what I thought." She rolled her eyes and clutched her large belly. "You just wait until I see that man." Her hand sliced through the air like a guillotine and Taariq jumped when a phantom pain shot through his crown jewels. This woman wasn't playing. Hell. At this moment, Charlie wasn't exactly at the top of his Christmas list either.

"Arrrrghh!" Gisella squatted so low she was practically on the floor.

"What are you doing?"

In between her grunting and panting, she looked up at Taariq as if he'd just sprouted two more heads. "What the hell does it look like I'm doing? I'm about to have a baby."

"But—but you can't have it here. We have to get you to the hospital." He moved forward and tried to take her by the elbow. However, she tried to grab his injured hand again. For a few seconds they looked like a comedy act with her hands looking like Wile E. Coyote and his hands racing around hers like the Road Runner. Finally she gave up and just started smacking him on the arm.

"Oww." He tried to duck out of the way from the sudden assault. "What are you doing?"

"I hate men! You did this to me!"

There was a loud gasp and both Gisella and Taariq's heads whipped toward the living room's archway where Anna stood with her eyes wide in shock. "What the hell is going on in here?"

Chapter 10

Taariq jerked as if he had been sucker punched by her sudden appearance. It was a strange reaction to a woman he'd determined was certifiable. And what was she wearing? She seemed to go out of her way to cover whatever curves her tall frame possessed. Today she wore a conservative black skirt and white blouse. Her jet-black hair was even pulled back into a tight bun, reminiscent of a strict schoolmarm.

Not his type, especially with the whole crazy, throwing-drinks-in-people's-faces thing.

So why couldn't he stop staring?

"Oh, thank God you came," Gisella said and then immediately burst into tears.

Anna's beautiful brown eyes narrowed with silent accusation before she raced to her sobbing sister. "It's okay. I'm here now." She knelt down and gathered her sister into her arms. "Are you having contractions?"

Gisella whimpered and nodded her head.

"How far apart?"

Her answer was a low guttural growl that Anna and Taariq couldn't understand.

Anna whipped her head back toward Taariq and asked him. "How far?"

He stood there like a deer caught in headlights.

"Hello?" Anna waved and snapped her fingers to jar him out of his trance. *"Is anybody there?"*

Taariq's spine stiffened. "Yes. I don't know what you want me to tell you. I don't know anything about contractions. I've been too busy trying to get her out to the car so I can take her to the hospital."

Anna huffed and rolled her eyes.

What in the hell do they want from me? I'm trying to do them a favor.

Gisella stopped grunting and went back to her *Hoos* and *Hees.*

"Okay. Did the pain just pass?"

"Y-yes. Hoo."

Anna glanced at the dainty watch on her wrist. "All right. Let's try to get you out to the car before the next one hits. Do you think you can do that?"

Gisella looked like she wanted to say no, but instead she nodded and allowed her sister to help her to stand back up.

"Well." Taariq clapped his hands together and took a step backward. "It looks like you have everything under control now." After all, this was a family issue.

"Where are you going?" Anna's accusing stare nailed him.

"I, um, well, er…"

"You're not going to leave me to do this by myself, are you?"

Well, not anymore. "Of course not. I was just—" his

gaze swept over to the suitcase "—going to grab her stuff," he lied with a shrug and then rushed over for the bag.

Anna's stern expression refused to relax while she watched him grab her sister's suitcase. Instinctively, she didn't trust Taariq. She never really had. In fact, it wouldn't surprise her one bit if he was really planning to jet out of there and leave her to deal with getting Gisella to the hospital by herself. He had made it clear that he wasn't the kind of man who stuck around.

"Aaarrrrgh," Gisella screamed and grabbed her sister's hand.

At the crushing pain, Anna dropped like a stone with her mouth sagging open in a silent scream. In a flash, Taariq raced over to try to help loosen Gisella's death grip, but he wasn't making much headway.

"Gisella, baby. I'm going to need you to let go," Taariq said, straining to lift just one finger.

If she wasn't in so much physical pain, she probably would've found this scene amusing with the strong muscular man struggling to overpower a petite Gisella—and losing. But since she *was* in pain, the situation wasn't funny at all. Bright multi-colored stars danced around Anna's head like a cartoon and it wasn't until Gisella's contraction passed that she was finally able to pry her hand free.

Anna stared at her crushed hand. "Oh. My. God!"

Sympathetic, Taariq turned toward her. "Are you all right?"

"Hell, no, I'm not all right. Look at my hand!" She thrust it in front of his face.

In response, he showed her his own warped-looking hand. "Trust me. I know exactly how you feel."

"Guys! Guys! Here comes another one," Gisella warned. She tried to grab hold of one of their hands again, but this time *both* of them scrambled out of the way, leaving Gisella to grab hold of a floor lamp and shake the hell out of it.

Anna glanced at her watch. "Wow. They're really coming pretty fast. I don't know if we're going to have enough time to get her to the hospital. We might have to deliver the baby here."

This time Taariq's head spun around so fast he nearly gave himself whiplash. "What the hell you talking about, Willis?"

Cradling her hands on her hips, Anna leveled a hard glare on him. "What do you think I'm talking about?"

"Do you know how to deliver a baby?"

She shifted uncomfortably on her feet. "Well, no. But—"

"But nothing. We're getting her to the hospital and that's all there is to it."

"The contractions—"

"All that means is that we just need to hurry." He rushed back over to Gisella as if the matter had been settled. Without pausing, he swept Gisella up into his arm like a groom would do his bride before crossing the threshold to their wedding night. The only thing that made it awkward was the fact that Gisella was still clutching the floor lamp. The result was her smacking him hard against his left temple with the iron pole.

"Oww." Taariq's knees dipped a bit, but he managed to regain his balance before they both tumbled to the floor.

"What are you doing?" Anna snapped. "Put her down!"

"No. You grab her suitcase and come on."

"I changed my mind," Gisella yelled. "I don't want to do this. I can't do this."

"Shh. Shh," Taariq said, trying to sound calmer than he looked or felt. "It's all right. We're going to get through this. We're going to get you to the hospital, if it's the last thing I do." He started toward the door and ignored it when she snatched the electrical cord out of the wall.

"Maybe she should put the lamp down," Anna suggested.

"Sure. Let's waste another five minutes trying to pry it out of her hands." Taariq rolled his eyes. It probably would take a miracle for him to get through this madness. He reached the front door and glanced back over his shoulder. "Are you coming?"

Anna bristled at his authoritative tone, but marched over to Gisella's suitcase. "We're not going to make it," she mumbled under her breath.

"Yes, we will," he countered.

She frowned at his supersonic hearing and the moment he turned his back, she couldn't resist making a face. Who in the hell did he think he was bossing her around? Her march transformed into a stomp as she followed behind them. When she pulled the front door closed behind her, she was surprised to see Taariq heading toward her car.

"I thought we were taking *your* car?"

"And possibly mess up my new car? Are you high?"

Anna jabbed a hand on her hip. "You can't be serious!"

He continued to stare at her, incredulous. "As a heart attack. Now are you going to unlock the door so we can get going?"

"Unbelievable." Anna hit the unlock button on her key chain and then continued her stomp toward the driver's side. The faster they got to the hospital, the faster this whole nightmare would end. When she hopped in behind the wheel, Taariq was finally trying to negotiate for Gisella to let go of the floor lamp.

"Please let go, Gisella. I can't get you *and* the lamp into the vehicle. *Please*."

"Hoo. Hee. Hoo. Hee."

"Yeah. That's right. Keep breathing—but let go of the lamp," he urged.

"Hoo. Hee. I want Charlie."

"I'll get him. I promise. We just have to get to the hospital first. Okay?"

Gisella looked as if she wanted to argue and cry at the same time. "I don't think I can do this."

"Of course you can," he said softly. "You're one of the strongest women I know. Literally. I have the broken hand to prove it." He winked.

Gisella actually chuckled but then started growling again when another contraction hit.

"Breathe," he reminded her. "Hoo. Hee. Hoo. Hee."

Gisella followed his lead and started her *hoo-heeing* again.

He smiled into her scared eyes and eased the tall lamp from her hands and set it aside on the front lawn. They continued their duet while Taariq eased her into the backseat of Anna's sleek SUV.

Grudgingly, Anna admitted to herself that she was impressed. Other than the fact that he didn't want to risk messing up his precious new Mercedes, he was actually coming across as a...decent guy—proof-positive that there were still miracles in the modern age.

Taariq had no idea how he was remaining cool. He just knew that it was important that he did. Once he placed Gisella on the backseat, he climbed in with her and shut the door. "All right. Let's go," he ordered, tapping the front seat. This whole thing was almost over. *Thank God*.

Anna turned the key, but nothing happened. "Oh, no. No. Not now!"

"What? What is it?"

Anna tried again. There was just a loud clicking sound and then—nothing. "I don't believe this. C'mon, baby." She leaned forward and kissed and caressed the steering wheel. "Start up for me, baby. Don't do this to momma."

Taariq hiked up a brow. "Do you two need a moment?"

"Shh," Anna hissed before whispering a prayer and trying again.

Nothing.

"Damn it!"

"Hoo. Hee. What is it?" Gisella asked, panicked.

Taariq smiled. "Nothing. Just keep breathing. Hoo. Hee," he repeated until she followed along. Slowly, he stood and leaned over the front seat to whisper to Anna. "What's up?"

"What do you think is up? The car is dead," she hissed. "We're going to have to take your car."

Taariq's calm, cool and collected face twisted.

"Oh, get over it, you big baby." She turned and hopped back out of the SUV.

He huffed and then rolled his eyes before turning his charming smile over to Gisella. "All right. Change of plans."

"What?" The worry lines returned to Gisella's face.

"Shh. Calm down. It's okay," he reassured. "We're just going to take my car."

"Oh, God. Charlie…" Tears rolled down her face.

Taariq's heart lurched, but he kept his smile firmly in place. "Don't you worry. I got you." He reached over and opened the car door again. Clearly this was the longest day ever created. Together they continued their duet while he carefully extracted her from the vehicle. However, when he carried her toward *his* car, tears suddenly stung his eyes.

I'll never forgive Charlie for this.

Since he'd left his keys in the car, Anna opened the backseat door for him. He paused for a moment while he wondered if he could place Gisella somewhere other than his leather seats. Unfortunately, that only left the roof or the trunk. For a few heart-pounding seconds, Taariq stared longingly at the trunk.

"Hello?" Anna snapped her fingers again. "Are you spacing out on me again?"

"What? No." He quickly delivered Gisella to the backseat of his car. "Don't you worry, G. I got you. I'll have you at the hospital before you know it."

Before Gisella could respond, she was immersed in the throes of another contraction. It was just bad luck that his ear got in the way. What the hell? It wasn't like he needed his hearing.

Taariq wiggled a finger in his ear as he shut the back door. Unfortunately, that didn't stop it from ringing. He started up the car and Anna jumped into the passenger seat and slammed the door.

"How soon do you think we can get there?"

"What?!"

Anna jumped. "Why in the hell are *you* yelling?"

He frowned. *"I'm not yelling!"*

She blinked at him and shook her head. "Let's just go."

He leaned closer. *"What? Why are you whispering?"*

"Just drive!" she screamed, ready to pull her hair out.

"Well, what did you think I was about to do?" Taariq shifted the car into Drive and slammed on the accelerator.

"Lord, give me strength," she mumbled as she reached for her seat belt.

Gisella continued to wail from the back. She called on Jesus and cursed Charlie's name almost in the same sentence. Her painful wail had Anna unbuckling her seat belt and climbing over the seat.

Taariq turned his head to see what she was doing and was pleasantly surprised at seeing Anna's butt two inches from his face. And what a nice butt it was—a thick upside down question mark that made his mouth water and his dick hard. How on earth did this beautiful butt get past him?

You're slipping, man.

A horn blared, forcing Taariq to turn his attention back to the road. He had less than a nanosecond to whip the car around a blue Corolla stopped at a traffic light. Anna and her nice butt rolled toward him while her long, dancerlike legs got tangled up with his hands and steering wheel.

"Ahh! What are you doing?" she screamed.

"Hold on!" The car veered to the right and she went rolling to the other side.

"Damn it. Are you trying to get us killed?" She went careening over the seats, but another sharp turn had her butt smacking Taariq's head.

"Hey! Watch what you're doing with that thing!" He shoved her butt out of his face and then gave her an extra shove so she could land face-first on the back floorboard.

At the loud *thump* he looked back in the rearview mirror. "Are you okay?"

"No!" Gisella and Anna shouted.

Taariq winced, and then felt ganged-up on. "All right. There's no need to shout!"

More horns blasted when he jetted in front of oncoming traffic and just missed getting T-boned by a large Ford F-150 truck that was barreling toward him on his right by mere inches.

"Oh, God. We're going to die," Gisella cried. In the next second, she was *hoo-heeing* like a runaway train.

Anna pulled herself up off the floor. "We're not going to die. We're going to be just fine." She didn't know why she said the words. Lord knew with Taariq's crazy driving, she hardly believed them herself. Smiling at her sister, she attempted to brush her sweat-drenched hair back from her face only for Gisella to seize hold of her hand and squeeze.

Anna yelped aloud while Gisella bent her knees and started pushing. "I—I don't think you should start pushing right now."

"Grrrrrrrr."

"Gisella, sweetie. Try not to push."

"Hoo. Hee. I—I can't help it. Grrrrr."

"Taariq, you better step on it," Anna said with panic strangling her voice.

"And just what do you think I'm doing?" He laid into his horn. "Move it, buddy!" *Honk. Honk.*

There was another hard swerve and Anna banged her head on the back door. Would this nightmare ever end?

"It's coming," Gisella announced before hunkering down and pushing again. "Grrrr."

Anna shouldn't have done it, but she leaned down to see what was happening and could literally see the top of the baby's head. *"Oh, God!"*

"What?" Taariq shouted from the front.

"Pull over!"

"Say what?"

"I said pull over!"

"But—"

"Now! Right now!"

Taariq jerked the wheel and pulled off the road. When he slammed on the brakes, everyone pitched forward. "What is it? Is something wrong?" he asked, turning around in his seat.

Anna helped push Gisella back on the seat. "Get back here. We need your help."

Taariq's antennae sprang up. "Me?" He inched backward. "What am I supposed to do?"

"I don't know. Come play catcher. The baby's head is coming through."

The mere though of that made Taariq light-headed. "But I'm not a doctor," he said, weakly. "I c-can't."

Gisella's scream reached a new octave. "Man up and get your butt back here," Anna snapped. Her eyes narrowed, giving Taariq the sneaky suspicion that if he didn't do as he was told that his own baby-making capabilities might be in danger.

A string of curses flew from under his breath as he turned and got out. While he stomped to the back of the car, he once again pictured wrapping his big hands around Charlie's neck and squeezing until he turned blue. It was a lovely fantasy. One that quickly ended when he jerked the back door open and saw what he felt no man should *ever* see.

Shortly after, he passed out cold.

Chapter 11

Charles Masters Junior was born at 12:01 p.m. in the back of Taariq's brand-new Mercedes-Benz. However, the owner of said vehicle was passed out on the side of the road while Junior's mother and aunt worked together to bring him into the world. A few minutes afterward, an ambulance pulled up and the paramedics took over.

Anna raced behind the paramedics as they wheeled *two* gurneys through the emergency room. This day couldn't have been more bizarre. She halfway expected Ashton Kutcher to jump out somewhere at any minute. However, that was highly unlikely.

"Ma'am, why don't you just stay with your husband for now? It's going to be a few minutes before we can get your sister and new nephew cleaned up."

"Husband?" Anna glanced down at Taariq lying on the gurney and then gave a short chuckle. "Oh, he's not my husband."

Taariq moaned and pressed a hand to his head. "Where am I?"

Anna rolled her eyes so hard it was amazing that they didn't fall out of her head and hit the floor. "We're at the hospital. No thanks to you." She glanced back up to talk to the nurse, but she was gone.

"What?" Taariq popped open his eyes and propped himself up on his elbows to take a good look around. "What happened?"

"What do you think happened? You fainted."

"Get out of here." He swung his legs over the side of the gurney and attempted to get up. "You don't know what you're talking about."

Anna lifted her brows and folded her arms. "So you think that you *magically* appeared at the hospital. Is that it?" The horror twisting Taariq's face was comical and Anna probably would have laughed if she wasn't so concerned about her baby sister that she hardly cracked a smile. How people believed that women were the weaker sex was beyond her. When he failed to come up with a response, she turned up her nose. "Well, thanks for nothing."

"Whoa. Hold up." Taariq hopped off the gurney. "I helped."

She leveled a *get real* look at him.

His mouth fell open when he realized that she was not about to give him *any* credit for the nightmarish hell he'd been through today. "Okay," he said calmly. "Maybe I did sort of choke when it was crunch time, but I wasn't expecting to see—" Taariq felt bile rise in his throat "—what I saw."

At the sight of him turning a puke-green, Anna shook her head. "Maybe you should lie back down. You don't look so good."

Taariq pressed a hand against his stomach. "I don't feel so hot, either."

Mildly concerned, Anna pressed a hand against his forehead, which didn't turn out to be such a good idea because it was like putting her hand into a roaring fire. The moment their skin touched, she had to snatch it back and even then her hand suffered from an invisible third-degree burn.

What the hell?

Whatever it was she was fairly certain that Taariq felt it as well because he was staring at her as if she'd suddenly sprouted two extra heads. The warning that sounded off sounded eerily like an air-raid alert. Instinct told her to turn and run away, but instead she stood firm and gave him a cynical smile. "You'll live."

Taariq's spine stiffened. What was it with this chick? Why was she always snapping his head off? "Look. I did the best I could under the circumstances. Would it hurt you to give me a little bit of credit?"

"What? Like bake you a cookie or something?"

He jerked back as if she'd slapped him. However, since he didn't know where all this anger was coming from with her, he just held up his hands to signal his surrender. "Whatever. I'm going to let you have that."

Anna sucked in a breath and realized that she was overreacting given the situation and she was likely coming off looking like a hysterical ninny. However, standing this close to Mr. Amnesia and pretending that she didn't loathe the very ground he walked on was too tall an order. "Now that you're back among the living, I'm going to go check on my sister and my new nephew." She turned but Taariq stopped her by grabbing hold of her arm.

"Nephew? She had a boy?"

Another heat wave rushed up her arm and her knees damn near folded. What unnerved her was that it was a different type of heat—one that tingled in a manner reminiscent of the pleasure she'd rather forget. Why not? He had.

"Yes. Gisella had a boy." Anna pulled her arm free and then pushed up her purse strap. "A beautiful baby boy."

"Yeah?" Taariq's lips curled into a smile. "That doesn't surprise me given that her mother is a knockout."

As if someone had snapped their fingers, Anna's smile evaporated. "Well, I better go."

Taariq frowned. Why couldn't he figure this woman out? "Yeah. All right." He sucked in a breath this time and looked around. There wasn't really any reason for him to hang out, but at the same time he didn't really want to leave. "Well, I guess I could check out the nursery and introduce myself to the newest member of the Masters family."

Disappointment rippled across her face before she had a chance to plaster on a smile. "I guess if you want to." She shrugged her shoulders. "I can't stop you."

He cocked his head. "But you want to?"

Her brief pause was answer enough, but she lied and said, "I don't really care what you do."

"I see," he answered, though he was more lost than he'd ever been. However, this time before he could question her, she'd spun on her heels and marched off. Still stunned, he stood there and watched her. Eventually his gaze drifted lazily down to her backside. She really did have a nice butt. He continued to stare when she stopped to talk to someone in hospital scrubs. After she pointed Anna in the right direction, Taariq waited to see whether Anna would glance back at him. He hoped that she would, mainly because he was starting to like getting under her skin.

Anna sashayed off, but just before she turned a corner, her gaze shot back at him.

Taariq lifted his hand and gave her a small wave. "Toodle-loo." He chuckled under his breath.

At that moment he wouldn't have been surprised to learn

that she was a master mouth-reader, given how hard she rolled her eyes before she disappeared. But even that tickled him. "What is your deal, Ms. Jacobs?" he wondered aloud. The only question now was whether he was curious enough to get to the bottom of it.

Chapter 12

For months Taariq had been dying to ask Stanley about how his date with Anna had gone or even if they were still seeing each other. But every time he practiced the question inside his head, he couldn't make it sound like he wasn't jealous—which he wasn't. He was just curious. There was nothing wrong with being curious.

The first football game of the season was being hosted at Derrick and Isabella's place and when he arrived, all of his boys' cars were already there. The day's game was the Steelers versus the Cowboys and there was no doubt that things were about to get rowdy since Derrick and Hylan were devoted Steelers fans while he and Charlie were die-hard Cowboy fanatics. Stanley wasn't that much into sports. He just tagged along to be around his buddies.

"Well, hello there, stranger," Isabella said, answering the door with a smile.

"Hello yourself, beautiful." Taariq leaned over and

planted a kiss on her cheek. "Is your knucklehead husband around?"

A roar of laughter blasted toward the front door.

Isabella rolled her eyes. "Does that answer your question?" She stepped back so that he could enter. "How have you been doing?"

"Doing good. I can't complain—or at least it doesn't do any good."

"Mmm-hmm. Sooo…are you seeing anybody yet?" she asked as she escorted him toward the living room.

"Uh, not at the moment. Why? Are you thinking about running away with me?" He winked.

Isabella popped him on his arm. "Not on your life."

Taariq laughed. "Just checking. You can't blame a brother for trying."

"I'm trying to be serious."

He shook his head. "Don't even go there."

"What?"

"Just because three of my buddies tossed in the towel doesn't mean that I'm crazy enough to do the same thing."

"Aw. C'mon now. You and Stanley don't want to be the last men standing, do you?"

"Yes. Absolutely. Positively. Yes!" His rich laughter deepened. "You'll have to pry my player's card out of my cold, dead hands."

"Yo, T! You finally made it." Derrick strolled away from of the sixty-five-inch flat screen to give him a knuckle bump. "You ready to get your butt kicked, man?"

"In your dreams!"

Hylan jumped into the fray and received his fist pound. "We'll see who's dreaming, man."

Charlie laughed. "Please, the Cowboys are going to smack that ass."

"You ready to put some money on that?" Derrick

challenged, heading back to the couch and the huge bowl of potato chips.

"Hell, yeah. Put your money where your mouth is, baby." Charlie and Derrick swung out their hands so that their palms slapped together and then gripped for a firm handshake. "How much we talking about?"

"The usual, man." Derrick said.

"You got it. Five dollars."

Derrick turned toward Hylan and Taariq. "Y'all want a piece of this?"

"Count me in," Taariq cheesed. "This will be like taking candy from a baby."

Gisella chuckled as she strolled out of the kitchen with a platter of hot wings. "Here you go, big ballers."

Charlie jumped up. "Here, baby. Let me help you with that." He grabbed the platter from her, stole a quick kiss and then sat it down on the coffee table.

Taariq settled into his usual chair and then tossed a glance over at Stanley who seemed to be on a personal mission to vacuum up an entire bowl of Chex Mix. "So how are you doing, Stan?"

"Same old. Same old." He chowed down another handful of party mix.

"That's good. That's good." *So have you and Anna gone out yet?* Taariq sucked in a deep breath but then turned his attention to the screen just as the Steelers kicked off.

A cell phone rang and Stanley stopped stuffing his face long enough to dig out his BlackBerry.

Taariq watched Stanley as he read the tiny screen and started texting. Was he texting Anna? Were they at the stage where they sent little cutesy messages back and forth? LOL. Smiley faces. He rolled his eyes at the thought.

Stanley chuckled and then kept texting.

"Want to let us in on what's so funny?" Taariq couldn't stop himself from asking.

"Oh, it's nothing. It's just—"

Charlie jumped up. "Go! Go! Go! Touchdown! Yeah!" He pumped his fists in the air. "This game is already a wrap." He rushed over to Taariq where he received another fist bump. "We're about to make some money, son."

Derrick shook his head. "Sit your loud butt down. This game is far from over."

Stanley shoved his phone back into his pocket and then climbed out of his chair. "I'm going for another beer. Anyone else want one?"

"Naw. I'm good," Derrick said.

"Me, too," Charlie followed up.

Damn. Taariq ground his back molars. Now if he asked about the text messages it would look like he was being nosey—which he wasn't. It was just…hell. He didn't know why the thought of Stanley and Anna together still gnawed at him. It just did. "I'll take a beer—but I'll come with you." Taariq stood up.

Stanley waved him off. "That's all right. I got it."

Annoyed, Taariq huffed out a breath and then eased back into his chair. A minute later, Stanley returned and handed him a beer.

"Thanks, man."

"Don't mention it." Stanley returned to his chair and reclaimed his bowl. "What I miss?"

"Steelers got the ball," Derrick answered, reaching for a hot wing.

Ding, dong.

Derrick looked up. "Who's that?"

The guys shrugged their shoulders but kept their faces glued to the television.

Derrick stood to go answer the door, but then Gisella rushed out of the kitchen with her son tucked under her arm. "I'll get it. It's probably just my sister," she said. "I invited her over."

Taariq felt a kick to his stomach before his gaze crashed into Stanley's. Each tried to read the other during the thirty seconds before they heard Anna's voice float from the front door.

"Sorry I'm late," she said.

"Girl, you're fine. Isabella and I are just getting started on those thank-you cards while the boys are watching football. Come on in."

"Oh, look at my little nephew. Hey, li'l Charlie."

The front door shut and then Taariq's heart started pounding when heard the women's footsteps heading toward the living room. *Be cool. Be cool.* He turned away from Stanley and tried to refocus on the game. Unfortunately, he couldn't get his brain to even comprehend what he was seeing on the screen.

"Hey, guys," Gisella called. "You all remember my sister, don't you?"

Derrick and Hylan looked up. "Yo, what's up?"

"Welcome to the family," Derrick added.

Charlie beamed. "Hey, sis."

Stanley stood and wiped the salt and grease onto his jeans. "Hello, Anna."

"Hey, Stanley." She smiled sweetly. "Look at you."

Gisella nodded. "Yeah. He's turning into a buffed Anderson Cooper."

Apparently that was all the invitation Stanley needed to stroll away from the rest of the boys so that he could get a hug. Taariq's ability to eavesdrop was thwarted when Derrick and Hylan jumped up from their seats. *"Go! Go! Go!"* But then their beloved quarterback got tackled so hard that he dropped the ball.

Derrick fell back onto the sofa. "Aw, man. This is some bull!"

Taariq missed all the action because he was still trying to peep what was going on with Anna and Stanley. But they were now walking toward the kitchen with the rest of the wives. Did he know that she was coming? Was that what all the texting was about? Taariq took a swig of beer while his gaze burned a hole in the back of Stanley's head.

"Taariq!"

"Hmm?" Suddenly, a throw pillow smacked him in his face. "What the hell?"

Derrick laughed. "Man, what the hell is wrong with you? Spacing out isn't going to get you out of paying me my money."

Hylan joined in. "Yeah. Well, we'll be expecting cash money."

Taariq took another swig of his beer. "It ain't over until the fat lady sings."

"What's that? You want to make this double or nothing?"

"Sure, whatever." Taariq shrugged.

"Whoa, ho, ho." Derrick and Hylan stood for another handshake. "You got yourself a bet!"

Charlie went all in, as well. "Now the game is getting interesting. Ten whole bucks." He laughed.

Taariq chanced another glance toward the kitchen, but Stanley and the women were no longer in his line of vision, which only made his imagination run wild.

"Anna, I'd like for you to meet Hylan's wife Nikki."

"Hello. Nice to meet you. I've heard so much about you."

Nikki blushed. "I hope it was flattering."

"Well, it was definitely interesting." Anna laughed.

"Yeah. Who would have ever thought that the best way to get a Kappa man down the aisle was to fake being married to him?" Isabella laughed.

Nikki laughed. "I guess I've always been a little... unconventional."

Gisella joined in. "Heck, I snared mine with chocolate—so go figure."

Anna zoned out when the married women started talking about babies. Her mind raced back to the man in the other room. *He didn't even acknowledge me.* Anna held her smile together while she bounced her two-month-old nephew on her knees. A small part of her said that she shouldn't care. So why did she?

"You know, I've been trying to call you," Stanley said, cutting into her thoughts.

Anna glanced over. She had forgotten that Stanley had followed them to the dining room. "I'm sorry, but work has been crazy lately."

"What is it that you do?" he inquired.

"I'm COO at the K & L Corporation. We're a management consulting firm. We have more than sixty offices in thirty-seven countries," she rattled off.

"Wow. I'm impressed." He smiled and bobbed his head. "You know, I'm not surprised that you're a success. I remember back when you used to tutor Charlie. Smart… and beautiful."

The other women fell silent as their heads whipped toward Anna and Stanley.

Anna blushed. "Thanks, Stanley. You're sweet."

Stanley groaned. "Oh, not sweet again. That's what you called me back in the day before you kicked me to the curb."

"You guys dated?" Gisella asked confused. "You never told me that."

"Oh, no. We never dated," Anna corrected. "He just…"

"Had a major crush on her back in college," Stanley filled in, his blue eyes dancing. "And then she broke my heart."

"I'm so sorry," Anna said.

"Oh, please don't feel bad. It was a long time ago." He cleared his throat. "But I'd still like to take you to dinner. You know, so that we can play catch up." By the time he got the question out, his entire face was red with embarrassment."

All eyes shifted toward Anna.

She hesitated because she still didn't feel that spark he wanted for him, but she couldn't bring herself to kick the same puppy twice. "I'd love to go to dinner with you." Anna leaned over and planted a kiss on his cheek.

The refrigerator door slammed shut and everyone at the table jumped and turned toward the kitchen. Taariq stood, holding up a beer. "Came for a refill."

Anna clamped her jaw shut and then gave Taariq the same silent treatment that he dished out.

"Well, try not to break my refrigerator door," Isabella said. "We just bought it."

"Sorry about that, Isabella." His gaze sliced toward Anna and Stanley before he turned and headed back out of the kitchen.

"I swear men don't realize how rough they can be with things some times," Isabella said, continuing to stuff envelopes.

"I'm learning that pretty fast myself," Gisella chimed in.

Li'l Charlie started squirming on Anna's lap and Gisella sprung into action. "Well, if you can excuse me, ladies," Stanley said, getting up from the table, "I guess I should get back to the game." He smiled down at Anna. "So what do you think about next Friday?"

Anna cleared her throat. "Ah. Friday's good."

A smile exploded across his face. "Great. I still have your card so I'll call you."

Anna nodded then watched him stroll out of the dining room.

"Well," Gisella said, grinning. "I guess your dry spell is finally over."

Anna shrugged. "I guess so."

Chapter 13

At halftime, the Cowboys were up 14-7, but one wouldn't know it judging by Taariq's lack of interest. Instead, he remained crouched over and shooting invisible daggers at the side of Stanley's head. Any attempt to try to examine exactly why he was angry was squashed internally because…well, just because. And anyway, he probably wouldn't be so annoyed if Stanley wasn't just sitting there, bobbing his head like the marching band on television was Jay-Z or something.

Suddenly, Taariq's dagger war was interrupted when Charlie stepped into his line of vision.

"Yo, T. Are you all right?" He thrust another cold beer into Taariq's hands. "You haven't said anything for the past hour. We're up seven points, man. Where's the love?"

"Oh, I'm cool." He forced what he hoped was a smile, but Charlie frowned as if he'd given him the bird. "What?"

Charlie shrugged. "That's what I'm trying to figure out." Slowly, he twisted around and glanced over at Stanley.

Stanley stopped rocking to the beat when he realized two sets of eyes were watching him. "What?"

"Nothing," Charlie said and then looked back at Taariq with a raised brow.

Taariq just ignored the silent question and took a long swig of beer.

"All righty then." Charlie strolled off just as Gisella appeared with her little bundle. "Hey, baby. Can you change Junior for me?"

Charlie accepted his son with a smile. "Not a problem. Whoo, boy. That's some ripe stuff you got going on in there."

"Don't talk about your son in front of company. You'll embarrass him." Gisella laughed.

Derrick strolled out of the kitchen and headed toward the deck. "Everybody staying for dinner later? I'm about to marinate these steaks."

"Count me in," Stanley hollered.

"What about you, T?"

"When have you known me to turn down a steak dinner?"

"Good point." Derrick laughed.

Taariq settled his gaze back on Stanley. All he saw was a replay of Anna leaning over and kissing him at the dining room table. Were they or were they not a couple? *What's the big deal? I just want to know.*

"Stanley," Anna said sweetly, coming out into the room while glancing down at her phone. "Can we move our date from Friday to Saturday? I forgot I'll be working late that day."

Stanley hopped out of his chair like a toasted Pop-Tart with an instant smile on his face. "Yeah. Saturday's great—same time?"

"Right. Eight o'clock." She flirted by tossing another smile at him, but before she turned away her gaze cut toward Taariq, whereupon she just lifted her chin and strolled off.

Once she marched out of the living room, Stanley chuckled under his breath. "Wow. She really can't stand you, man. Are you sure that you didn't do anything to her?"

"Positive," he grumbled.

"Well, all I know is your loss is my gain—and I don't say that too often."

Taariq took another long swig of beer while still trying to stop himself from examining his emotions, he was more than happy to pin his irritation on Stanley. He was as good a target as any. "Sooo. You have a date Saturday night? Here I was about to ask you to be my wingman this weekend," he baited.

"Sorry." Stanley smiled so wide that it nearly stretched from ear to ear. "But there's no way I'm breaking this date. It's taken too long to actually get her to agree to a date."

Taariq perked up, but reminded himself not to sound too interested. "So you guys haven't gone out yet?"

Stanley shook his head but his smile remained intact. "Nah. She's been too busy. But all that changes this weekend. I'm going to plan the perfect evening, man."

"Is that right?" Taariq turned up his bottle again while he could literally feel his blood pressure rise.

"The game's back on," Stanley shouted.

Hylan tore himself away from Nikki and raced back into the living room with a new tub of onion dip. "All right, Steelers. Let's even this score up!"

Charlie returned with the li'l man in tow. "Keep dreaming. We got this one, right, T?"

Once again, Taariq had to tear his eyes away from the side of Stanley's head and force them toward the screen. "Right."

"Well, don't sound too excited." Charlie laughed.

* * *

After two hours of flipping through wedding pictures and endless talks about what to expect when you're expecting, Anna was ready to call it a day. After all, there was only so much happiness a single girl could take. Sure, she was genuinely happy for her sister and her newfound sisterhood with Isabella and Nikki, but it was exhausting trying to beat back that little green-eyed monster that kept asking where her knight-in-shining-armor was.

Maybe it's Stanley. She silently shrugged and then weighed the possibility. She was impressed that he'd put about twenty pounds of muscle on his frame since she'd seen him at Gisella's wedding and the silvering of his hair really made his blue eyes pop. He was actually...quite handsome.

While she was thinking over the possibility of her and Stanley, Derrick popped up at the dining room door.

"Hey, babe. Me and the guys are going to toss the ball around before I throw the steaks on the grill."

"Is the game over with already?" Nikki asked.

"Yeah. Hylan and I are ten dollars closer to the poor-house, but we have a chance to make it back right now in a quick game of touch football."

"Alright. I'll put the steaks on the grill," Isabella said.

"No. I can do it in about twenty minutes," he said.

"Don't worry. I don't mind," she said, kissing him on the cheek. "You go on outside and play with your friends."

Derrick's face exploded with another smile. "Have I told you lately how much I love you?"

"Not for at least ten minutes." She kissed him again. "Now go!" She smacked him on his butt and he rushed off.

Anna watched the saccharine-sweet scene and then sighed longingly. *One day.*

"Come on, girls," Isabella said. "Let's move this party out to the deck."

"I think I'm going to go ahead and go," Anna said, standing up.

Immediately the women's faces collapsed in surprise and disappointment. "What? Noo," Gisella moaned. "Stay. We're all having such a good time."

"I know, but I have so much work to get done back at the house," she said with her usual excuse. In reality there was a pint of Häagen-Dazs ice cream in her freezer at home that was calling her name.

Gisella was having none of it. "Not today. You work too much. Today you're going to hang out with us and your little nephew." She eased the baby into Anna's arms.

"But—"

"But nothing. I don't want to hear it. The matter is settled." Gisella flashed a quick smile and then turned toward Isabella and Nikki. "Now let's take this little party out onto the deck."

The girls laughed at the sisters little scene and then climbed out of their chairs.

"Oh, Gisella, don't forget to give me the number of your obstetrician," Nikki said, patting her small belly as she trailed behind her.

Anna sucked in a deep breath as if it would miraculously give her strength to get through another round of exuberant baby talk. But then she looked down at her sleeping nephew and a smile instantly eased onto her lips. And a fresh wave of longing washed over her heart. He was so…perfect.

Wouldn't it be nice to have one of my own?

Little Charlie cooed softly in his sleep and then adjusted his head upon her chest, which caused her to fall deeper in love.

"You look like a natural."

Anna's head jerked up to see Taariq standing in the

doorway. He'd finally caught her alone again. She tensed and then the baby stirred in her arms. *Relax,* she coaxed herself. It was almost impossible, especially with Taariq casually leaning against the doorway and staring at her as if he was mentally stripping her clothes off. "What do you want?" she growled.

Taariq's expression didn't change, only a single brow lifted a fraction of an inch higher than the other one. "What makes you think that I want something?"

Put on the spot, Anna shifted her weight side-to-side while her entire body flushed with irritation. Unfortunately, Little Charlie picked up her changing mood and started squirming and fussing in her arms.

Taariq stepped forward. "Aww. You're upsetting little man."

Anna stepped back but bumped into the dining room table. "I'm not upsetting him. You are. Now just go away."

He ignored the request and instead reached down to run one of his fingers against the side of the baby's right cheek. "Shh, little man. Everything is going to be all right," he whispered softly.

The moment his finger made contact, the baby settled down with a soft sigh.

"What are you, the baby whisperer or something?"

"Or something."

When Taariq smiled, Anna's heart felt like it was skipping every other beat. He was standing too close, stealing her oxygen while she was pinned between him and the table. The baby luxuriated in his deep slumber, completely unaware that his aunt was fighting like hell not to start hyperventilating.

Anna tried to keep her focus on the baby and not look up. If she did, she feared being trapped in Taariq's dark gaze.

"So when are you going to tell me why you hate me so

much?" Taariq asked, his voice staying soft as a lullaby. But he'd asked the wrong question and Anna's gaze jumped up with a new fire.

"You *know* why," she spat in a low voice.

Taariq's forehead creased with confusion just as Stanley bolted into the room.

"Hey, T…" He stopped while his gaze took in the idyllic scene between Anna, Taariq and the baby and his eyes narrowed with suspicion.

"Yeah, man. What's up?" Taariq asked, removing his hand and stepping away from Anna and the baby.

"Me and the boys are ready to toss the ball around outside. You coming?"

"You're playing?" Taariq asked, surprised.

Stanley pumped up his chest. "Yeah, man. You know that I like roughing it up with the fellahs." He cast a nervous smile over to Anna. "Are you coming outside, too?"

"Looks that way," she said, taking full advantage of the opportunity to escape around the human wall that was Taariq. Even as she forced her legs to carry her out of the dining room, she could still feel Taariq's heavy gaze follow her to the backyard deck.

"What are you doing, man?" Stanley asked.

Taariq tore his eyes away from Anna's back and shifted them over to an annoyed Stanley. "What?"

Stanley shook his head as he stared at his friend. But he didn't press the issue. Instead, he calmly turned around and marched off.

Taariq drew in a deep breath and then hustled out to join the others.

The men gathered out in the yard for a light game of touch football. They were all more than a little surprised that Stanley wanted to jump into the mix. Regardless of his recent twenty-pound muscle gain, the last time anyone checked, Stanley hardly knew how to even throw a football, let alone had the coordination to run or catch. But after seeing him constantly looking up toward the deck where the women sat and watched, it was clear that Stanley was hoping to impress Anna.

Taariq's irritation flared again. And when he threw the first pass, maybe he threw it just a little too hard. Stanley's arms came up too late and the ball nailed him in the head.

Stanley emitted a high-pitched yelp and then went down for the count.

"Awww, daaaammmn!" The men winced at how hard Stanley hit the ground.

"I'm okay. I'm okay." Stanley sat on the ground for a moment and tried to shake it off.

Taariq jogged over. "You all right, man?" He offered his Kappa brother his hand, but Stanley grabbed Charlie's and Derrick's to help pull him up.

"I'm good."

"You're going to have to get your arms up faster than that if you're going to play with the big boys," Taariq warned.

Stanley nailed him with a hard look. "I'll keep that in mind."

"All right." Hylan laughed. "Shake it off." They all rushed back to the game.

Stanley took a moment to wave up to Anna to let her know that he was all right.

Taariq rolled his eyes and went back to getting his hustle on. The next time Stanley got the ball, it was Charlie doing a soft pass off before instructing him to "Run!"

For a half second, Stanley had a deer-in-headlights look before finally getting his feet to move, but by then Taariq was bearing down on him so hard that he literally looked like a locomotive about to run down a baby fawn.

Stanley glanced over his shoulder and saw his fate about a second before it hit him. Again, there was another high-pitched scream shortly before he had a mouth full of grass.

"Oooooh!" The other brothers covered their mouths and shook their heads.

"That hurt me just looking at it," Hylan said, jogging over to check out the damage. "You all right, man?"

"I'm...I'm..."

Taariq trotted back and hovered above Stanley as he rolled over onto his back. "Good hustle, man," Taariq praised with a thin smile.

Stanley couldn't respond. He was too busy trying to suck in enough air to breathe.

"Damn, T. Does the brother owe you money or something?" Derrick and Charlie reached down, but Stanley lacked the upper body strength to pull himself up so they had to stoop down and pick him up.

Charlie frowned once Derrick and Hylan lifted Stanley by holding one arm and leg apiece. "You don't look so good."

Stanley winced. "I think something is broken."

"C'mon, man. You're all right." Taariq reached up and ruffled his silver hair. "Just shake it off."

"Ahh." Stanley winced again when the guys attempted to help him stand up.

Charlie shook his head. "Maybe we should get him to the doctor?"

"Is he all right?" Isabella yelled from the deck.

Taariq looked up and saw all the women on the edge of the deck, trying to assess what was going on. Now he truly felt like an ass. He tried to laugh it off. "C'mon, a doctor? I barely touched him."

The guys laughed at that.

"C'mon," Derrick said. "Let's get you to the emergency room."

Taariq still had a hard time believing that he caused his brother that much damage. "He's fine," he repeated, following the guys back toward the deck.

Stanley elected to milk the situation by moaning like he was seconds away from seeing the Grim Reaper. Once they reached the back deck, Anna rushed over to take a long look herself.

"Stanley, are you all right?"

He moaned relentlessly. "I don't know. There might be some internal bleeding."

"Oh, please." Taariq rolled his eyes. "He's faking it."

All the women's gazes shot over to Taariq and he squirmed under their silent accusation. "What?"

Derrick and Hylan carried Stanley into the house.

Anna seized the moment. "You could've seriously hurt him! What were you trying to prove? That you're bigger and stronger than he is? Is that how you get your rocks off? You run over people to get what you want and then never call him again? Huh? Is that it?" She stabbed him in the middle of his chest with an acrylic nail and he held up his hands to signal his surrender. "You know what you are? Just a big, callous, insensitive bully and I hate the day I met you!" She spun on her heels and marched off. "I have to go."

Everyone's mouth dropped open as she stormed back into the house. Once she was gone everyone's eyes zoned in on Taariq.

He was left looking as stunned as the rest of them. "No offense, Gisella, but I think your sister is missing a few screws." He marched into the house. It was definitely time to leave.

Charlie glanced over at his wife. "What was all that about?"

To his surprise, Gisella smiled. "If I didn't know any better...I'd think that those two like each other."

Chapter 14

"I want to set my sister up with Taariq," Gisella announced, easing into the bed next to her husband.

"Come again?" Charlie snapped the mystery novel that he was reading closed.

"Well, I think she needs someone and..."

"You think Taariq's the guy for her, even after the way she blew up at him today?" He laughed as he reached out and turned off the lamp. "I don't know, honey. I think that you're barking up the wrong tree on that one." He turned so that he could spoon her.

"Why? Taariq is nice, plus he's handsome and successful. He'd be perfect."

Charlie frowned. "He's also a die-hard bachelor. It's not going to be easy to pry the player card out of his hands."

"I got your card."

"That was different."

"Why? Because you thought that you were dying?"

"Low blow, baby." He kissed the back of her head. "So

what you're saying is that we have to convince Taariq that he's dying so that he can take stock of his life and decide to settle down?"

"No." She tapped him on the arm. "All it takes for a man to want to settle down is to meet the right woman, right?"

Charlie didn't answer.

"Right, baby?" she insisted.

"Sure. Right. Whatever you say, baby." He pressed another kiss against her head.

"It may not be easy, but it's not impossible either," she said. "Again, look at you."

"I'm not a good example. You drugged me with chocolate."

"What?" She popped him on the arm. "You take that back."

Charlie laughed and snuggled a kiss in the crook of his wife's neck until she started giggling.

"Baby, stop. You're going to make me wake up the baby."

"Oh. We don't want that." He slid his arm up and cupped her breasts. "I plan on working on getting him a little brother or sister tonight."

Gisella giggled some more, but then refused to give up on her brilliant idea. "C'mon, sweetie. What do you really think about setting them up? I'm just worried about my sister. I don't like the idea of it being just her and her cat Sasha for the rest of her life. She deserves to find someone. I want her to be happy."

Charlie moaned at having his best moves being shut down. "I want her to be happy, too, if it makes you happy—but Taariq, baby? I don't want you to get your hopes up. Besides, Stanley likes her. He'd been trying to get a date with her all summer and now that he fractured his leg, he's bummed about having to cancel their date this weekend."

Gisella mulled his answer over while he went back to work nuzzling her neck. "Don't get me wrong. I like Stanley, but I don't think he's the guy for Anna. She needs… an alpha male. Someone who's strong and aggressive but still knows how to be kind, funny and sweet."

Charlie's kisses dried up. "Kind, funny and sweet? Since when have you started checking out Taariq?"

"Oh, calm down. I told you that I'm looking for someone for Anna, and Taariq is perfect. Is he going on the ski trip?"

"I don't know. I just asked Derrick and Hylan. I thought you just wanted it to be a couples thing." He shrugged.

"I do. Taariq and Anna will make the fourth couple."

Charlie shook his head. "I don't know. I'm not too comfortable with this whole matchmaking thing. Plus, Anna didn't look all that crazy about Taariq to me. I'm afraid if we leave those two alone that yellow crime tape might be needed by the end of the night."

"If anything goes wrong you can just blame me and say that you told me so."

Charlie's head popped up at that. "Do you really mean it?" Quickly, he rolled back over to his nightstand, clicked on the light and grabbed a pen and paper. "Do you mind putting this in writing?"

Gisella laughed and then rolled back over to her side of the bed.

Charlie tried to thrust the pen and paper at her. "Baby?"

"Good night, Charlie."

"Wait. I'm just saying that this moment needs to be documented in time."

"I said good night, Charlie." She hid a smile in her pillow as her husband finally gave up and turned out the light.

* * *

Anna couldn't sleep.

Sitting out on her balcony and sipping on warm milk while Sasha purred and bathed herself on her lap, she reviewed everything that had happened that day. Now that her temper had finally settled, she reflected on how she had stormed out of Derrick and Isabella's place like a fire-breathing dragon. Surely they all thought that she was off her rocker by now. Yet at the same time, Taariq just got under her skin like nobody's business. And the fact that he kept acting like he hadn't done anything wrong was completely mind-boggling.

Why can't he just say that he's sorry? If he's sorry. Why act like she was the crazy one in this? But the look on his face while she was screaming and yelling was really something else. She couldn't imagine too many women putting that big, muscle-head oaf in his place—or that he stuck around long enough to hear it. There was a definite satisfaction in telling him off, even if she didn't get the answer to a question that had been floating in her head for a long time.

"Why do you care? It was so long ago," she whispered under her breath. Hell, she had gone years not thinking about Taariq and that night. Then again, maybe it was because he was out of sight and out of mind. Now with Charlie married to Gisella, the arrogant jerk was orbiting her life and popping up when she least expected it.

Just tell Gisella that you no longer want to be around him. That suggestion sounded simple enough, but it no doubt would require her having to tell her sister why she didn't want to be around one of her husband's best friends. And what would she say? The truth was a bit humiliating, which is why she had never told anyone about that night. She could try to lie, but she had never been a good liar.

Anna sucked in a long deep breath and let her mind

roam while she stroked Sasha's soft coat. And of course her treacherous mind zoomed right back to Taariq and her standing in Isabella's dining room with li'l Charlie nestled in her arms. He really did have a way with babies. *I wonder if he has children of his own?* Of course that would mean that he had some baby mommas floating around Atlanta.

She rolled her eyes at that. Wouldn't that be typical? Anna shifted in her seat, not liking the idea of him having children already. She shook the image out of her head, but it was quickly replaced with another one—Taariq running across the backyard looking like a sleek, black panther with long, strong strides that quite literally took her breath away.

Her mind looped that image for at least a good hour. By that time she realized that she'd better take her butt to bed. If she was lucky she would get at least three hours of sleep. However, once she'd curled up against her pillow and Sasha took her place at the foot of the bed, any hope she had of escaping dreams of Taariq went out the window. He was right there waiting for her the moment she closed her eyes. It had been a long time, but she tried to remember every moment of their one night together. Amazingly, she still remembered what he tasted like. How remarkable was that? And the way his hand had roamed up her leg when they were on the dance floor at the frat party, she was certain that she hadn't experienced anything even remotely that hot in all her years of dating.

But when it came to that wonderful time in her dorm room, well, that felt more like a dream—even after all these years. It was just too bad that he hadn't felt that way, too.

Because if he had he would've stuck around.

Chapter 15

A week later, the Lonely Hearts book club crowded into Anna's living room. All of them seemed ready to bust at the seams with the latest dirt on their struggling love lives. Well, everyone except for Anna. Like always, she was content to just play hostess by making sure that everyone's coffee cups remained full.

"First, I'd like to make an announcement—I'm going back into the closet," Emmadonna said.

"Well, at least it lasted longer than I thought," Ivy sniped. "What was that—three months? I gave you three hours."

Jade laughed. "I had three minutes."

"It might as well have been three minutes," Emmadonna said. "It's not like I roped in a girlfriend or anything. I've been to one gay bar and, child, it's a hot mess up in those places, you hear me? How come lesbians aren't as fashion forward as gay men? Child, what I saw up in there was a crying shame."

"So you're running back to the other team because you didn't like their clothing?"

"That…and I just wasn't feeling it. I need muscles, broad shoulders, thick thighs and a schlong that can rock my butt to sleep. You feel me?"

A snapshot of Taariq flashed in Anna's mind and she accidentally burned her tongue on her coffee.

"Shi—" She glanced up. "Sorry. It's hot."

"Anyway," Emmadonna continued, "I walked my butt out of that lesbian bar and I ran up on this fine *papí* down at The Atrium. Girl, now those Columbian men are where it's at!" She held up her hand and went around the room until everyone gave her a high five.

"Oh, here she goes." Jade laughed. "She's done found herself another nationality."

"Shoot. I believe in exploring *all* my options. Ain't going to find me sixty-five caring for a bunch of cats."

Sasha meowed from her perch on the ottoman.

"No offense," Emmadonna tacked on.

Meow.

Anna chuckled and tried another sip of coffee.

"So you guys want to hear what's going been going on with me and Reece?" Ivy said.

"Who?" Anna and Jade asked in sync.

"You know, Reece." She rolled her hand along. "The Mandingo god I met at Gisella's wedding."

"Oh, yeah." Three smiles stretched across their faces.

Ivy rolled her eyes and folded her arms. That was never a good sign. "Well, everything was cool…until his technically still married butt got arrested for owing child support."

"What?"

"Uh-huh, girls. We were just coming out of Piccadilly after meeting my parents."

"Whoa," Anna said. "You actually introduced him to your parents?"

Ivy shrugged. "Hell, I really thought his broke butt was the one. Turns out he's got a wife and twin boys stashed in Jamaica that he conveniently forgot to tell me about. Can you believe these brothers out here nowadays?"

"Yes, I can," Jade said, rocking her head and crossing her legs. "I finally had to let Harold go when I realized that he had developed quite the habit of leaving his wallet at home every time we went out for dinner. Sometimes I swear all of these men are just looking for a sugar momma. They want us to do everything. There's no effort anymore."

Anna heard her friends talking, but she really wasn't listening. She was trying to list all the things that she imagined were wrong with Taariq. The main one being that he clearly enjoyed having one-night stands where he crept out of bed before the sun rose. Then there was the possibility of him having a slew of baby mommas and illegitimate children running around all over Atlanta. Hell, he probably didn't even know about them since he never stuck around to see if he'd knocked someone up.

"Anna! Anna!" Emmadonna started snapping her fingers in front of Anna's face.

"Huh? What?" She blinked out of her reverie to see that everyone was staring at her. "Do you all need a refill?" She started to stand.

"Nah, girl. We were asking what's up with you. Have you gone out with that white boy yet? Or is he the reason that you're zoning out over there?"

Anna laughed. "No. Actually, Stanley and I haven't gone out yet. His leg is still in a cast."

"What? What happened?" Ivy asked.

Anna shrugged while the image of Taariq's hard tackle flashed in her mind. *Those legs. Those muscles.*

"Anna?" Jade probed.

"Oh, um. He and his boys were playing football and he got tackled pretty hard."

"Huh. I would have never thought of Stanley as the athletic type," Emmadonna commented, nonchalantly.

Anna had to laugh. "He isn't. I think he was trying to impress me."

"Aww. That's sweet." Jade rubbed her shoulder. "I can't remember the last time a man tried to impress me—other than my daddy."

There was a circle of agreement.

"You're still going to go out once he gets better, right?"

"Yeah, sure." Anna shrugged. "I don't see why not."

"You better," Emmadonna warned. "A lady never turns down a free meal."

"And neither do some of these brothers out here," Jade chirped.

The women laughed just as the doorbell rang.

"Be right back." Anna hopped up and rushed toward the door. "Gisella? What are you doing here?"

"Would you believe that I was just in the neighborhood?" She plopped a kiss on her sister's cheek and then entered the apartment. At the sound of the Lonely Hearts laughing in the living room she made a beeline to go join them.

"Ah, Gisella!" All the women jumped to their feet to give her a hug.

"Where's that adorable baby of yours?" Jade asked.

"He's at the barbershop with his father," Gisella answered.

"Isn't it a little early for a haircut?" Anna laughed, coming up behind her.

"Yes. But you know that Herman's is Charlie's hangout spot and he wanted the fellahs to meet his son. Male bonding is what I think he's calling it."

"Well, look at you," Emmadonna said, holding Gisella's arms out. "Your little body just snapped right back into shape. You can't even tell that you were pregnant. You make me sick," she said with a smile.

"Sorry, babe."

While Gisella said her hellos, Anna went into the kitchen and made her sister a cup of coffee, just the way she liked it. "Here you go," she said, returning to the living room.

"Thanks." Gisella accepted her cup of coffee and then took a spot on the sofa next to Ivy.

"Soooo. Are you just here for a visit or are you looking to rejoin our little group?"

"Not unless you guys are actually going to start reading books."

The girls all looked at each other and then chorused, "Naaaah." They erupted into another round of laughter.

"I didn't think so." Gisella rolled her eyes and then focused her attention on Anna. "You know that ski trip is coming up."

The sudden change in topic jarred Anna for a moment. "Ski trip?"

"Yeah. Remember I told you that Charlie and I wanted to plan a vacation trip that could include family and friends?"

"Oh, yeah. That sounds nice. You guys will probably have a good time."

"You guys? You're coming, too."

"Me?" Anna frowned. "I thought you said that this was like a couple's thing? I'm not dating anyone right now and I definitely don't want to be that one pathetic odd girl out while everyone is being all lovey-dovey with each other." She shook her head. "Nah. I'll pass."

"Pass? Why? You're not going to be doing anything— and it's not just going to be couples. There will be other single people there."

Anna's hackles rose. "Like who?"

Gisella hesitated. "Like people. What does it matter? I want you to come with me."

That explanation did nothing to alleviate her suspicion. "Gisella, I don't know. You know that I have a lot of—"

"Don't tell me that you have to work. You have vacation time. You're coming."

Anna could be just as stubborn as her sister, especially since Charlie's friends included Taariq. "I can't."

"Why?"

"I just…I don't want to," she insisted.

"Does this have something to do with Taariq?" Gisella asked.

The other girls' ears perked up.

"What? No," Anna lied. "Why would I care about Taariq going? This has nothing to do with him." Her face grew warm because she suspected that everyone knew that she was lying.

"Well, good. 'Cause he's not going," Gisella said. "I think that he has other plans with some…body."

"With who?" Anna asked before she could stop herself.

Gisella shrugged with a soft smile. "Who knows? You know how the Kappa men are. And I doubt that Stanley's going to be able to go because of his leg."

Anna had stopped listening after Gisella had said that Taariq was going to be spending time with some mystery chick. Who was she? Was it serious? What did serious mean to Taariq?

"Anna! Anna!" Gisella snapped her fingers in front of Anna's face.

"Huh? What?"

Gisella frowned. "What's with you?"

"Actually, she's been doing that a lot lately," Emmadonna said.

"I was just…thinking."

"So you'll go?" Gisella said. "We haven't been on a vacation together since we were little."

Anna sucked in a long breath. "All right. I'll go."

"Great!" Gisella jumped up then gave her sister a tight hug. "You're not going to regret this. I promise."

Anna returned the hug, but in her mind, she still wondered who Taariq was seeing.

The moment Charlie strolled into Herman's Barbershop with his little mini-me nestled in a baby carrier against his chest all the men who'd had their faces glued to SportsCenter hopped up to check out the latest member of their boys' club.

"Oh, he looks like his momma," Herman said. "Thank God."

The brothers got a good laugh at that.

"Check it out. Check it out." J.T. reached into his mobile merchandise coat and pulled out a gold chain. "I got something for little man."

Charlie pulled away. "J.T., don't give my son none of that cheap junk. That stuff may be liable to turn green and poison him."

"Nah. Nah. This is the real deal. I got this from a friend of a friend's cousin that swears this stuff is legit."

"Man, if you don't get on with that mess…" Charlie moved past the brother and headed over to one of the available chairs. No sooner had he sat down did Derrick, Hylan and Taariq stroll in. They received their rounds of celebratory greetings before heading to their seats.

"Well, well, well. If it ain't Charlie and his little shadow," Taariq said, strutting over. "Looks like you have this whole papa thing down." He held up his fist for his usual knuckle bump, and then tweaked the baby's cheek. "It looks like your momma's good looks saved you."

Charlie rolled his eyes. "There's a joke that never gets old."

Taariq chuckled and then took his place in Bobby's chair.

"You're a good role model," Derrick said. "I hope I turn out half as good as you. Right now I'm just trying to survive Isabella's mood swings. She's all sweet and cuddly one minute and the next she's all weepy and crying because I painted the baby room banana-yellow instead of sunshine-yellow."

Hylan chuckled. "I think I'm ahead of the game because my wife was arguably insane before I married her so I haven't detected any real mood swings."

The boys chuckled.

"I always thought that it would take a special kind of crazy to put up with you," Derrick added.

"I'd second that." Charlie laughed.

"Ha. Ha. Nikki is wonderful and she's going to make a great mother."

"How's her play coming along?" Charlie asked.

"So far, so good. She found a director and they'll be doing casting soon. Hopefully everything will come together by the spring. If the play does well here in Atlanta, then she'll look at touring and eventually landing on Broadway—at least closer to Broadway than the last time. By the way, thank you all for investing. It really means a lot to me."

"It's no problem, dog. Now that Masters Holdings has climbed out of debt, I'm glad to do what I can. Speaking of which, are you guys still going to be able to go on the ski trip?"

"Actually, I've been meaning to get back with you on that," Derrick said. "We're going to have to back out. The whole skiing while pregnant doesn't exactly sound like a wise thing to be doing."

"Same here," Hylan said. "Maybe we can do it next year?"

Charlie bobbed his head and before turning his attention to Taariq. "What about you? You can't ski while pregnant, too?"

"Very funny. I don't have any babies here or on the way."

"So you're coming?"

He hesitated.

"C'mon, man. You don't have anything else to do and since you landed our man Stanley on some crutches, it's not like he's going to be able to go. I'd hate for it to be just the three of us."

"You're taking the baby?"

"Nah. My mother will be watching my little man here. So far it's looking like it's going to be just me, Gisella and Anna."

Taariq's eyebrows sprung up. "Anna is going?"

"Yep. Gisella is determined to get her out and about. She's afraid that she's working too hard and not enjoying life." Charlie shrugged. "I'm starting to agree with her."

Taariq shifted in his chair. Maybe he could get Anna off alone somewhere so that he could find out once and for all why she hated him so much. He was tired of trying to figure it out on his own. He wasn't used to getting such vitriol from women. They usually loved him.

"Taariq! Taariq!" Charlie snapped his fingers in front of his boy's face.

"Huh? What?" Taariq snapped out of his reverie. "What were we talking about?"

"The trip. Are you in or are you out, man?"

Chapter 16

By the first of the year, Anna had studied everything she could on backcountry skiing. Last time she'd gone skiing she was sixteen. Her father thought it would be a good idea for his daughters to bond on a trip to Austria. They did. Anna picked up the sport rather easily, but now it had been so long she felt like she needed a refresher course. As with everything that she did, she wanted to be knowledgeable about anything and everything she tried to do. Not only did she study everything that she could get her hands on, she must've bought over half the items in the sporting goods store. She didn't want to get caught not having something.

Of course, the look on Charlie's face when he and her sister showed up at her condo to load up the SUV was comical.

"I...don't think that we're going to be able to take all of this." He walked around the pile in the living room, scratching his head. "You know that we're just going for the weekend, right?"

Anna nodded and tried to imagine what in her four-foot pile of luggage and equipment she could leave behind. "I'm sure that you can get it to fit."

"But what is all of this stuff? Backpack, sleeping bags… and what is this?" He reached for something that looked like it had handlebars.

Anna leaned over. "Oh. That's a snow bike."

Charlie cocked his head at her. "What the hell do you need a snow bike for?"

"Well…I had read on the internet—"

"Stop. Stop." He held up his hand. "It stays," he announced.

Anna opened her mouth to protest, but her brother-in-law gave her a stern look that made it clear that he wasn't playing. "In fact, why don't you and Gisella go on down to the car and I'll weed out what can go and what will stay?"

"But—"

Gisella grabbed her sister's arm. "Let's go, Anna. Let him figure this out. Trust me." Gisella laughed. "Let him figure it out before you give him a heart attack."

Anna finally allowed her sister to push her out of the condo. An hour later, Charlie had the SUV loaded to the max before he climbed in behind the wheel.

"All righty. Let's get this show on the road," Charlie said, flashing Anna a mini-smile through the rearview mirror. Then they were off. They made it to the airport in record time and when Charlie started loading up his private plane, Anna looked around.

"So where is everybody?"

"Hmm?"

It was a strange reaction since Anna was looking dead at Gisella when she asked the question. "I asked where is everybody?"

"Oh. Um. Isabella and Nikki aren't going to be able to make it. The whole pregnancy thing."

"I thought that was a little odd, but then I thought they were just going to hang around the lodge and sip cocoa."

"That would've been nice, but the whole high-altitude and everything… Next time, we're going to have to pick something that doesn't involve a whole lot of physical activity since we'll never know who will be pregnant at any given time."

Anna's eyebrows stretched at the hidden implication. "Does that mean that you guys are planning on more children soon?"

Gisella's face lit up. "Maybe. We'll see."

Laughing, the women climbed aboard the airplane. Once in the air, Gisella went on about how fabulous married life had turned out and bragged about how well Sinful Chocolate was doing even during the deep recession. Again, Anna felt happy for her sister, but recognized the growing hole in her life. The hole she kept filling with work and episodes of *CSI: Miami*. After a while, she doubted Gisella even noticed that she had stopped commenting on all the cute little things she and Charlie did to keep the romance alive in their marriage. Gisella was content with just her smiles and constant nodding.

At some point she turned toward the window and stared out among the clouds. It, too, had a way of isolating and illuminating the loneliness she felt. *Cheer up. You're on vacation. You're going to have a good time.* She sucked in a deep breath and stretched her smile a little wider. It was hard because she was going to be just what she didn't want: a third wheel.

* * *

The spectacular vistas of Powder Mountain instantly captured Anna's imagination. It was over seven thousand acres covering three mountains and Anna had read that the place had more than a hundred and thirty-five runs so that there was no fear of having to deal with crowds.

The white alpine mountains were postcard perfect and the air was so crisp it gave her a natural high. Now she was actually looking forward to tackling the hiking and ski trails. The Deer Mountain resort rented slope-side ski lodges with sweeping views of a number of trails. Powder Mountain averaged five hundred inches of snow and had ski-terrain ranges from plow-deep powder backcountry to finely groomed corduroy for beginners to advanced-level skiers.

However, one could never quite plan for the cold. In just a couple of seconds after stepping out of the yellow Hummer rental, Anna was freezing.

"Oh, my God!" Thick white clouds puffed around her face as she sucked in the thin air.

Gisella was moving as fast as she could when they made a mad dash for the door.

"I take it that I'm not going to get that much help with the bags?" Charlie laughed.

"We'll see you inside, honey," Gisella yelled without a backward glance. Once they were inside the lodge, they immediately doubled over and sighed as if they hadn't been around heat in eons.

"Good evening. May I help you?" a chirpy blond behind the front desk inquired.

"Ah, yes." Gisella headed over to the desk with Anna trailing behind. "We have a reservation under Masters."

The woman pulled open a thick book and then ran her fingers down a long column. "Ah, Masters. We have you down for two cabins."

"Oh, ah…" Gisella turned toward her sister. "We made the reservation when we thought a few more people were coming. Maybe we should just get one and ask for a cot?"

"No. No. That's all right. I'll take the other cabin by myself."

"Are you sure?"

"Yeah. Of course." The last thing Anna wanted to be was a third wheel inside a newlywed's room, and they were still technically newlyweds.

Gisella cocked her head with one of those sympathy smiles married women usually gave brave singles whenever they flashed their independence. The resort's lone valet finally rushed out and helped Charlie lug in all the bags.

Anna thought that there had to be some mistake when Charlie only brought three bags to her room. She had to have packed at least twelve bags, but given the exhausted look on Charlie's face she simply smiled and thanked him. Once she was alone, she headed straight over to the queen-size bed and fell across it, face-first. Her moment of solace only lasted for a few minutes before her phone rang.

"So you want to try to hit the slopes before dinner or do you just want to get situated and then head to dinner?" Gisella asked excitedly. With it already being late afternoon, Anna figured that they only had an hour before the sun took a nosedive. "Situated and then dinner," she decided and realized that she had said the right answer when she heard Charlie's "Thank God" in the background.

"All right. I'll call you back in…let's say, two hours?"

"Sounds good." Anna hung up and then glanced around her big spacious cabin and could feel the solitude creep back into her bones.

Taariq struggled to keep his cool while he watched Delta post delay after delay for his flight to Utah. Had he not had an important meeting at his firm today then he would have flown out with Charlie and the family. As it was now, he was stuck at Hartsfield-Jackson Airport hoping and begging for a standby ticket. He did everything he could think of—charm, cajole and even bribe the woman behind the ticket counter.

When a seat finally became available, he was ready to leap up like he'd suddenly gotten the Holy Ghost. However, when he calculated his estimated time of arrival, he realized that he probably wouldn't make it out to the ski resort until damn near two in the morning. Still, it would be worth it if he could finally get to the bottom of this animosity that Anna had toward him.

It was still a mystery why it bothered him so much. He wasn't one of those people who had to have people like him. He wasn't a vain egomaniac or anything. Far from it. Maybe once he got some answers, he could stop dreaming and obsessing over her.

When he woke up in the morning, he thought about her.

When he was preparing depositions, he thought about her.

When he was with the boys, he thought about her.

And, of course, when he went to bed at night, he thought about her.

Taariq had to go on this trip and confront Anna once and for all. This whole thing was messing up his mojo. Hell, he hadn't been on a date in months and if Stanley ever took her out on a date, he was afraid that he would send his boy back to the hospital. How screwed up was that?

During the whole flight, Taariq kept practicing in his head how he'd go about approaching Anna about this situation. With it just being the four of them, it wasn't like she could simply avoid him—not easily anyway. He'd play it cool and try not to upset her too much, even though she seemed easily upsetable.

He thought about it some more. Maybe he was more like Hylan than he thought? He was attracted to slightly crazy women, too. *Attracted.* That word kept popping up even though Anna's whole conservative vibe wasn't something he normally went for.

She didn't always dress like that. A vision of nineteen-year-old Anna standing at a frat party dressed in a tight black dress that left little to the imagination flashed in his mind. She had legs that went for days and an elegant collarbone that begged him to plant a string of kisses across it. The memory brought a smile to his face. There was a lot he liked about that night…and a lot he regretted.

Dinner was as uncomfortable as Anna had feared it would be. There were more baby and adorable marital stories than Anna knew what to do with. Plus, Gisella had the need to keep calling Charlie's mother to check in or remind her mother-in-law of junior's little idiosyncrasies, like needing to sleep with his favorite blankie or what song to sing when rocking him to sleep.

She loved her sister and Charlie, but it was all starting to be too much. The one thing she was looking forward to was hitting the slopes in the morning. By the end of dinner, it was clear that they were all exhausted and ready to head back up to their cabins.

After a nice long shower, Anna pinned up her hair and put on a cool avocado mask and then worked a healthy dose of cocoa butter into her skin before climbing into bed and turning on her waterfall CD. She thought about reading, but exhaustion finally settled in and she was out like a light before she knew it.

At exactly 2:00 a.m. Taariq climbed out of a freezing cab at the Deer Mountain resort. He'd only managed to take two steps before he hit a sheet of black ice and his legs went flying out from under him.

"Oomph!" He landed flat on his back and smacked his head.

"Sir! Are you all right?" The cab driver rushed around the vehicle.

Since every ounce of air had evacuated his entire body, it took Taariq a moment to clear his head. "Yeah, I think I'm all right." He attempted to move, but pain, unbelievable pain ricocheted in places he had long forgotten about. It took some work, but with the cab driver's help, they managed to peel him off the ground. Of course, he ended up hobbling into the resort like an old man in need of a walker.

Taariq tapped the bell on the counter until an older white gentleman in a thick blue-checkered robe shuffled from around the corner.

"Morning," he said, then coughed to clear his throat. "You're coming in rather early."

"Or late," Taariq corrected. "I'm with the Masters's party. They should've checked in earlier today."

The older gentleman pulled out a pair of lined bifocals from his pocket and then opened a thick ledger to scroll for the name. "Masters. Masters. Masters—oh, here we are. Party of four, two cabins." He turned around to a big board and pulled out a key. "Here you go. Cabin 4. I'll just need for you to sign your big John Hancock right here and right here."

Taariq took the pen and signed for the key. He needed to hold it together for just a few more minutes and then he could collapse into a nice big bed and put this entire day behind him. Tomorrow he'd figure out a plan to talk to Anna.

Chapter 17

Getting to cabin 4 required another trip outside through the blistering cold and invisible ice patches. Taariq experienced a few close calls where he nearly slipped and slid, but with his ingenius use of helicopter arms, he managed to stay on his feet. But he'd never felt more relieved than when he finally reached his destination. He nearly melted on the spot when he entered the cabin's welcoming warmth. The difference from being outside and inside was the equivalent of heaven and hell. Hopefully it would be a little warmer in the morning.

Seeing the roaring fire, Taariq pulled off his gloves and made a beeline over to the glowing flames so that he could warm up faster. "Good ole Charlie," he mumbled under his breath. He must have stood there for a good ten minutes with his hands held out as close to the fire as he could possibly get before feeling comfortable enough to strip out of two layers of clothes. Next, he dug out a few items from his bags and went straight to the bathroom for a thirty-minute steaming-hot shower.

Anna stirred gently in the bed before curling away from the bathroom door; she didn't pick up on the subtle change in the relaxing sounds of her waterfall CD. Instead she just barreled deeper underneath the covers and released a dreamy sigh when an image of Taariq floated across her head. In her dreams it was impossible for her to hold on to her anger. In fact the only thing that they seemed able to do in her fantasies was tear each other's clothes off.

In dreams was also where Anna truly let her hair down like she did that one night so long ago....

In tonight's fantasy she wore a sexy black silk number with lace peekaboo sides. When she stood posing before Taariq's greedy eyes, she could see his pleasure by his rising erection in his black briefs.

"Do you like?" she asked him, spinning around.

"Like? I love." He moved toward her with the strong, muscled legs that she loved so much and pulled her into his arms.

Anna tossed her hair back with a throaty laugh and he instantly went to work raining kisses down her long neck and across her scented collarbone...

By the time Taariq shut off the shower the entire bathroom was one big steam room. At least this frozen hellhole had a great water heater. He grabbed one of the towels and proceeded to wipe the condensation from the mirror. He briefly checked out his side profiles. It was important that he brought his A-game tomorrow when he saw Anna.

"Now how could she say no to this face?" he asked himself. It was meant to be a confidence booster because Anna had been saying no for a while now. Taariq glanced down at his body. He flexed his pec muscles one at a time. *I still got it.*

He turned from the mirror and continued to pat the remaining moisture from his body. When he exited the bathroom, he saw something move in the bed and heard the sound of falling water.

"What the hell are you listening to, man?" He shook his head. Married life must've really changed his brother if he was reduced to listening to mood music to fall asleep. Then he glanced around and frowned. "Why on earth did you book one bed?"

No response.

The brother must really be tired. Taariq strolled back over to his bags while he wrapped his towel around his waist. Hopefully, he didn't forget to pack some pajamas. But the more he thought about it, he didn't really own any pajamas.

Anna squirmed underneath the covers....

Taariq had her body pressed against him while his large hands roamed freely over her soft skin and sexy lingerie. Bumping up against her butt was his still-growing erection. She hesitated to even guess how big it was now. She just knew that she liked the way that it teased her through their thin clothing—so much so that she started rotating her hips and pushing back up on it.

"Hmm. Now what are you trying to do?" *He let her work it for a bit.*

Anna listened to how his breathing changed and even how he dropped a few moans. Meanwhile, his hands kept roaming and caressing until they worked their way up and had her full breasts pressed into the palms of his hands—then it was her turn to start moaning.

"Ah. You like that, do you?"

"Mmm-hmm." *She leaned her head back in a way that*

gave him easy access to her neck. He instantly picked up on the hint and lowered his lips to plant those wonderful kisses.

When her moans grew louder, Taariq gave her breasts gentle squeezes until her nipples poked out like marbles. "Now let me see what we're working with tonight."

There was a brief wave of disappointment, but that disappeared the moment he tugged down the thin straps of her dainty teddy. Suddenly those lips started moving south and landed on one of her exposed shoulders. His hands returned to her breasts. This time it was flesh against flesh.

Anna sucked in a ragged breath and struggled to keep her legs from collapsing underneath her. The slow seduction started fraying the edges of her sanity. She wanted this torture to end and end soon.

Taariq slipped on a fresh pair of boxers and glanced back over at the bed. Was Charlie having a bad dream? *Probably thinks that he's dying again.* He chuckled under his breath and then moved over to the sofa. Him and his boy were tight, but he wasn't about to climb into bed with him. He plopped down and then gathered a couple of throw pillows together. The room was at a decent temperature so he didn't bother searching for any covers. He was just content to lay his aching body down in front of the dying fire and go to sleep.

But that only worked for about five minutes. *What is this sofa made of—bricks?* There was no way that he could sleep on that damn thing. He glanced up at the bed, but still wasn't cool with the idea of sharing a bed with his longtime buddy. Of course, the other option was the floor.

"Good Lord." *Can this day get any worse?* Heaving in frustration, Taariq climbed to his feet and shuffled over to the bed. Now that the flames in the fireplace had faded to just glowing embers, the cabin had plunged into total darkness. The only sounds were the howling winds outside and that crazy waterfall CD playing from the clock radio on the other side of the bed. "Don't take this the wrong way, brother. But I'm just not that into you." He grabbed two pillows from his side of the bed and lined them in the center of the bed before climbing into it.

Taariq sighed contentedly as he melted into the fluffy pillow-top and tucked his last remaining pillow under his head. Immediately afterward, his eyes drifted close and a vision of Anna greeted him...

One foot away from him, Anna's mouth sagged against the pillow....

Taariq slowly turned her body around so that his head and kisses could continue their southern descent. His tongue flicked wickedly against her hard nipple once... twice and then he gently sucked it in whole between his lips.

"Mmm." She grasped his head, making it clear that she wanted him to stay right there. Anna could feel him smile against her breasts. That was okay as long as he continued his wonderful suckling.

In the meantime, Taariq's hands were still busy working their magic, peeling her black teddy down over the curves of her hips and then letting it fall the rest of the way to the floor. He finished putting a glossy coat on one nipple and then turned his head so that he could go to work on the other one.

Anna's grip loosened slightly so that he could maneuver but she was now losing herself to the feel of his hands traveling up her trembling thighs.

"Open up for me," he whispered.

He certainly didn't have to ask twice. Anna took a single step to the side and Taariq's large probing fingers slid across the silky hairs lining her brown lips. Without having to be asked, she widened her stance.

Taariq chuckled at her open eagerness but also wanted to give her a reward. He sprang his mouth off her delicious nipple and then moved his head to the valley between her twin peaks and then slowly unrolled his glistening pink tongue and let it glide all the way down the center of her body...

On the other side of the bed...

Taariq envisioned him and Anna standing beneath a spotlight in the center of the dance floor. She appeared as a goddess in a sleek, sexy, one-shoulder red dress. He stood before her in a black tux and, from behind his back, produced a single red rose with a short stem. She smiled and Taariq slid the rose into the strands on the left side of her head.

"Beautiful," he whispered.

Anna smiled demurely and then allowed him to lift her hands in position. Suddenly an invisible DJ threw on some hot Latin music and off they danced in a dizzying and hypnotic rhythm. Even though in the recesses of his mind he knew that he didn't know how to salsa dance, in his dream, he moved like he'd been dancing like this...with her...for forever.

It didn't make sense, but yet it was so perfect. They were perfect.

Soon, he was spinning her around like a bottle top. When she finally came to rest in his arms, both were out of breath and staring into each other's eyes as though they were trying to get lost in them.

"Why do you hate me so much?" he asked.

"I don't hate you," she answered, smiling. "I love you. I've always loved you."

Her words were like music to his ears, even though the

conscious part of himself knew that it was just a lie. Their invisible DJ slowed the music down and they were reduced to just swaying to a simple two-step.

"It's been a long time since we've danced," Taariq whispered against her ear.

"Yes. It's been way too long." She pressed her head against the side of his face and started humming in tune to the romantic melody circling them.

"You know...if you want...we could dance like this for the rest of our lives." He inhaled a deep breath when he realized what he was saying—that here was a woman that he could truly see spending the rest of his life with. Here was a woman who effortlessly intrigued him and challenged his entire belief system, and it didn't scare the hell out of him. "How does that sound to you, sweetheart?"

He tilted his head back so that he could see and hear her response. To his delight, her face lit up with a glowing love that took his breath away.

"I would love to dance with you forever," she whispered, drowning in his eyes.

Taariq leaned down and sealed the deal with a kiss. But it was no ordinary kiss. This one made him feel as if he were sailing through the sky or that he was the king of the world, King Kong or even perhaps the Lion King. Maybe love did that to a man, it made him feel strong and indestructible.

For a long while, he was content to just drink from her lips, but then he could feel her small fingers start to undo the buttons lining the front of his shirt. His response was to deepen their kiss while he went to work on the tiny zipper on the back of her dress...

On Anna's side of the bed, she began to toss around in her sleep....

Taariq's hands stopped their slow glide between her

legs, but only so that his index finger could penetrate easily through her wetness. Her head eased back as her body erupted with tiny tremors and a slow wave of honey slid down between her legs.

"Ah. Look at you. All nice and wet for me," he whispered and then stirred his fingers around.

Anna's hammering heartbeat mirrored that of her pulsing clit that beat back against Taariq's stirring finger. As a result, she neared her first orgasm in no time at all.

"That's it. Let it go," Taariq coaxed, sliding in his middle finger and hitting the right spots at the right time.

"Ahhh." Anna's legs trembled and their ability to hold her weight remained unstable. That is, until Taariq's fingers split open into a V and exposed her honey-coated pearl.

Taariq watched as her pretty pink clit transformed into a dark cherry while she neared her second orgasm. When he was convinced that she was ripe enough, he leaned forward and glided his tongue along its pounding base...

In bed, Anna turned and smacked into a small wall of pillows. Yet no alarms went off inside her head. She was too lost in what was happening inside of her mind that she simply grabbed one of the pillows and tucked it in between her legs. Unfortunately it did little to help the ache that was growing in reality, so she grabbed the other pillow separating her and Taariq and clung to it as she turned over in bed.

Meanwhile, Taariq's dream was just heating up....

After peeling off Anna's red dress, Taariq was delight-fully surprised and turned on to see her wearing a sexy black silk number with lace peekaboo sides. His steel-like erection stretched another inch, making him impatient to be inside of her. He took his time, stroking and caressing her soft skin.

Anna moaned.

Taariq smiled.

After enjoying his eye candy for a moment, Taariq wasted no time in stripping Anna out of her sexy lingerie. Next he wanted to concentrate on raining kisses from the top of her head all the way down to the soles of her feet....

Anna's hands clutched Taariq's head like her life depended on it while he continued to feast from her body's nectar until her knees finally gave out. Only then he laughed at her flushed face.

"I take it that you liked that, baby?"

She hid her smile in the crook of his neck. "You know I did."

Gently, Taariq raked his fingers through her hair. "What do you say that we continue this over on the bed?" He pulled her head back so that he could nibble on her lips and share her taste.

"I'd love that," she whispered, licking her lips.

Together they stood and strolled over to the king-size bed. She leaned back and he climbed on top. He immediately zeroed in on his favorite spot: the soft curve at the base of her neck...

Sighing, Anna released the pillow she held in her arms and rolled over toward the real Taariq in her bed just as he turned toward her. Their bodies met in the center of the bed. Neither of them thought anything of the added sense of smell: her fragrant hair and his male-scented soap. If anything it only heightened their libidos and fed their unconscious desires.

When Taariq started peppering *real* kisses along Anna's sensitive collarbone, she responded by curling toward him and moaning softly into the night. Loving the melodious sound, he sought her lips while his hands slid down her body. Damn, she tasted good and he was sure that he could truly taste her spearmint lips. This had to be the best damn dream that he'd ever had.

He absently pushed the pillow away that was tucked between her legs and replaced it with his hands. Even when he discovered her silky wet panties, he didn't question it. He just tugged them off with one swift pull and then kneed her legs farther apart.

Anna thrashed her head away from Taariq's hungry mouth for some much needed oxygen. But the ache between her legs was such an unbearable torture that she begged, "Please, Taariq. I need you now."

Taariq knew exactly the kind of pain that she was in because he was experiencing it himself. He removed his briefs as if Houdini was his middle name. And when his cock pressed against her entry, her legs came up greedily and locked around his hips. With that, there was only one direction to go. Holding her hips, Taariq eased slowly in between her warm, slick and tight walls.

Ecstasy like he'd never known took hold of him and refused to let go—not that he ever wanted to. With that one thrust, he could feel everything. Her breath. Her heartbeat. And a long-neglected need that he was now determined to fill.

In sync, their bodies moved in a mating dance that was as old as time itself. Their joining was an instant connection like two long-lost pieces to a forgotten puzzle.

"Yes…yes…" Anna moaned as real tears started rolling from the corners of her eyes. Nothing in her life had ever felt this glorious. The way the man made her body hum and her mind spin was something that she knew she could absolutely get addicted to. As a bright light started to glow from behind her closed eyes, she effortlessly surrendered her body and soul to the power that was building up inside of her.

When it exploded, she cried while Taariq growled mightily against her ear. Afterward, Anna was sure that she'd splintered into a million pieces, but all that mattered was that she was content…and satisfied. She was vaguely aware of a few more kisses as Taariq gathered her close and tucked her against his chest.

When they finally slipped into a deeper stage of sleep, one thought was threaded between them: Why couldn't this night have been real?

Chapter 18

Riiiing! Riiiing!

Anna moaned and snuggled deeper into the crook of Taariq's arm. She inhaled his now-familiar scent and slid on a soft smile. Peace and contentment radiated through her body. Somehow she had found heaven in this one comfortable spot in the center of the bed. For a fleeting moment, she found herself wishing that she could spend the entire ski trip lying right there.

Riiiing! Riiiing!

"Oh, God. Make them go away," she complained.

Taariq groaned. "Maybe if we just ignore them they will."

Anna nodded and burrowed deeper into her warm alcove.

At long last, as if picking up on the hint, the phone stopped ringing.

"See? What did I tell you?" Taariq slid an arm over the curve of her hip and then pulled her tighter.

A lazy smile drifted over Anna's face, but slowly her brain started to churn. *Was I just talking to someone?* A few more spokes got in on the act and her curiosity grew. *Maybe I'm still dreaming.* She lay between the worlds of reality and dreamland while trying to figure out which way to go. However, now that her curiosity had been stirred, her other senses started to tune in. The first was her sense of smell. The seductive fragrance that she'd fallen in love with sometime during the night seemed a little too real. Next was her sense of taste. She swore that there was a lingering foreign taste on her tongue that she didn't quite recognize. Then it was her hearing, besides the sound of crashing waterfalls streaming from the CD player, there was the slow, steady sound of someone breathing.

For a crazy moment, she held her breath—but the mysterious breathing continued and was in sync to the same rhythm as whatever she was leaning against. Her heart stopped.

Open your eyes. She was too scared. What if there really was someone in her bed?

That's impossible. There can't be anyone in here. The very idea that some mystery psychopath had broken into her cabin in the middle of the night terrified her so much that her heartbeat went from zero to sixty in a snap.

Open your eyes! Anna started praying as her lashes fluttered and she opened her eyes one millimeter at a time. Her heartbeat slammed on the brakes again when a muscular, black chest came into focus. If there was any consolation at least her mystery psycho had a nice chest. Her eyes lowered to how the bed's sheet was casually draped across his nicely cut hips. And what was that hardening against her thigh?

She slammed her eyes shut. *I'mdreamingI'mdreaming I'mdreaming.* Maybe if she said it enough times then it would be true. It had to be true. For a full minute, Anna clung to that slimmest of possibilities with everything she had. But it wasn't working. There was just one more way for her to be sure. She reached down and grabbed the back of her hand and twisted. The instant pain brought reality in sharp focus.

This time her eyes flew open. When the same muscular chest greeted her, she jumped up and scrambled backward, screaming at the top of her lungs.

Taariq bolted straight up like a soldier responding to an air raid. *"What? What's going on? What happened?"* His gaze flew across the bed and took in the wild-haired and green-faced screaming banshee. He yelled out in fright and then tipped over the side of the bed. His body hit the floor with a thud, but his head cracked against the nightstand, knocking him out cold.

At the sickening sound, Anna stopped screaming. *Was that Taariq?* She jumped out of bed, clutching the top sheet and then raced around to see if he was all right. He landed at an odd angle and she immediately feared the worst.

"Taariq!" She dropped to the floor and shook him by his shoulder. When he continued to lie there like a crash-test dummy, she lowered her head against his chest and then checked for a pulse on his wrist. She relaxed a bit when she found a strong pulse.

Anna sat back on her haunches and then started tapping him on the face. The taps became slaps and he finally started to stir. "Taariq, wake up, damn it, so I can cuss you out."

He moaned and his long lashes fluttered.

Anna jabbed her hands onto her hips and waited until his dark eyes focused. "Are you finished trying to kill yourself?"

Taariq jumped and tried to scramble back again.

"What the hell is wrong with you now?"

"Anna?"

"Who in the hell did you think it was? And what the hell are you doing in my cabin?"

"I don't know. What the hell is that on your face?"

Anna's hands shot up to touch her face and at the feel of its rock-hard mask that she'd put on before going to bed, she screamed and then bolted toward the bathroom.

"Good. Now you know how I felt," he mumbled just before she slammed the door shut.

Anna took one look at her reflection and just barely swallowed another scream. Her hair was all over her head. And the mask on her face was the color of day-old guacamole. No wonder Taariq had been scared out of his mind. She doubled over at the sink and turned the water on to full blast where she scrubbed, rubbed and rinsed her face for a good twenty minutes. When she finally patted her skin dry, it was as soft and smooth as a baby's bottom.

After that, she took in the rest of her appearance, most importantly the wetness in between her thighs. There was absolutely no doubt in her mind that she had had sex last night. She knew in a way that a woman could always tell. She met her gaze in the mirror and tried to figure out how she felt about this latest development. Being honest with herself, she wasn't particularly angry as much as she was just confused.

"I know who, what and when…I just need to figure out how and why." She glanced at the closed bathroom door, but wasn't ready to march out, demand answers and hurl accusations. Maybe she wasn't ready for them.

Drawing in another deep breath, Anna turned toward the shower. She turned the water on full blast and was stunned by the immediate boiling-hot temperature. Quickly, she adjusted the dials before her skin was peeled off and then reached for the liquid soap. She had doused her entire soap sponge and started scrubbing before she recognized the masculine cologne soap.

"Ugh!" She tossed the sponge aside and reached for the other bottle behind Taariq's and then tried her best to scrub his scent from her body. She didn't miss how tender her breast felt or how delectably sore she was between her legs. As she continued to wash and rinse, snatches of a dream flashed in her mind.

"But it was a dream," she whispered and then shook her head. None of this was making any sense.

After using half a bottle of mango and apple soap and being damn near pickled, Anna finally shut off the water and climbed out of the shower. She took her time, patting and then wrapping the towel around her body. She even stalled for additional ten minutes by running the brush through her hair. *You can't stay in here forever.*

Anna expelled a long breath, set the brush down and went back out to finally get some answers. When she pulled open the door, Taariq sat waiting on the edge of the bed in just a pair of black boxers and still rubbing the back of his head.

"Are you all right?" she asked, timidly.

Taariq looked up and flashed a flat smile. "I think I'll live. How are you doing?"

She shifted her weight and leaned against the frame of the door with a casualness that she didn't feel. "I'm good."

He bobbed his head. Silence filled the space between them, each waited and wanted the other to speak first.

"All right," Anna said, drawing in a deep breath. "I'll go first. What are you doing in my room?"

"I didn't know it was your room. I thought you were Charlie."

Anna's mouth fell open.

"Whoa! Wait! That didn't come out right," he said, standing and shaking his head. "I don't mean that I thought

that…you know that I did what I did because I thought…
that you were…him. That's not what I'm saying."

Watching his face turn completely purple, Anna closed
her mouth. "Then what are you saying?"

"Okay." He lowered his hands. "When I arrived last
night, I did think that Charlie and I were sharing a cabin.
He said something about the guys having one cabin and the
women another. So when I got here, I just assumed—"

"Okay. I got that part." She rolled her hand.

"Well, then I came in, took a shower…started to lie
on the sofa, but it was way too uncomfortable because I
busted my butt outside when I got here so I got in the bed.
But I remember putting pillows in the middle of the bed,
thinking that would be a barrier between us, but I guess
not…"

Anna allowed that explanation to hang in the air between
them. Then she said flatly, "We had sex last night."

Taariq nodded. "I, uh…figured that much out."

"I'm not quite sure whether it was consensual."

He jerked. "Wait, now. I'm pretty sure that I didn't force
myself onto you."

"How do you know?"

"How do you know that you didn't jump me?"

Anna rolled her eyes. "Oh, please. I would never make
that mistake *again*."

Taariq's face twisted with confusion. "Again?"

Riiiing! Riiiing!

Anna rolled her eyes and then marched over and
snatched up the phone.

"Oh, Anna! You're finally up."

"Yeah. I'm up." She glanced over at Taariq who was still
frowning. "I'm also *not* alone."

"What do you mean?"

"Charlie's boy Taariq showed up in the middle of the
night."

"Oh."

"Yeah. For some reason he was under the impression that he and Charlie would be sharing a cabin." That explanation didn't make much sense. Why would a married couple split up?

"Oh."

Anna frowned at her sister's noncommittal answer. Suddenly a thread of suspicion pricked at the back of her head. She turned and gave Taariq her back. "You didn't know anything about this, did you?"

"Know anything about what?"

Anna thought that she was trying too hard to sound innocent. "Gisella, you shouldn't have. You don't know what you've done."

"Done? Why, what happened?"

Anna sucked in a deep breath and shook her head. Gisella was playing matchmaker. The last thing Anna was about to confess was that she accidentally had sex with a man she couldn't stand. "Nothing." She shook it off. The thing to do now was to make sure Taariq got his own cabin. "Forget about it. I'm about to get dressed and I'll just meet you and Charlie for breakfast."

"That's what I was calling you about. Have you looked outside?"

Anna made another turn toward the window, but the blinds were closed and the curtains were drawn. "No. Why?"

"Because we're snowed in. I doubt that you'd even be able to get out of your cabin. We're in the middle of a blizzard."

"A blizzard?"

Anna and Taariq turned toward the window. He raced over, pulled back the curtains and opened the blinds. What

they saw made their mouths drop open. A wall of snow
was piled to the middle of the window.

   "Oh. My. God." She was trapped...alone...with Taariq.

Chapter 19

An hour later, Anna had finished putting on two layers of clothes and went to stand in front of the window. In her hand, she sipped from a piping hot cup of cocoa and marveled at the sight in front of her. "I don't think I've ever seen so much snow."

"That makes two of us," Taariq said, exiting the bathroom, fully dressed in jeans and a black turtleneck. "A couple more inches and I think the entire cabin will be completely buried."

"Buried alive. That's a humbling thought." She shook her head. "I saw online that this place gets about five hundred inches a year—who knew that it was all at one time?"

Taariq laughed. "Any more hot cocoa?"

"Yeah." She turned and nodded toward the lone coffee-maker. "There's plenty over there, plus there's a ton of canned food and battery-operated appliances in the little kitchenette. This resort is prepared for this type of thing apparently."

Taariq nodded. "Good to know. I can put off panicking for a little while."

Anna smiled and resumed sipping her hot cocoa. Now that they'd exhausted their conversation about the weather, what was left for them to talk about? *Oh, hey. Did you know that my sister and brother-in-law tricked us into sharing a cabin?* That was not a conversation that she wanted to have. She returned her attention to the snow-covered window.

She didn't hear Taariq coming up behind her, but she recognized his scent as he drew near. Trying to appear casual, she took a giant step to the side.

"I'm not going to bite you, you know."

"Hmm?" Anna turned, hoping against hope that she pulled off an innocent look.

She didn't.

Taariq chuckled at her lame attempt and shook his head. "I said I'm not going to bite you."

Next, she tried to smile but that didn't work out so well either.

To prove his point, Taariq held up his hands and took an equally giant step back. "I'm not the bogeyman, Anna. Try to relax." He walked over to the coffeemaker and proceeded to make his own hot cocoa. "I'm at a loss as to how last night happened, as well. Though I do have a theory."

Anna lifted her brows. "You do?"

Taariq nodded. "Would you like to hear it?"

Shifting her weight to one side, she cocked her head. "I'm dying to hear it."

"I thought you might." He stirred the powdered cocoa. "Last night…I had a rather interesting…dream."

"A dream," she repeated, feeling her neck grow hot when flashes of her own erotic dream played inside her head.

"Yeah. It began innocently enough."

"What was it about?" she asked, her voice raspy.

The corners of Taariq's lips inched upward. "It was actually about...you."

She swallowed. "Me?"

He nodded, his eyes now holding hers prisoner. "If I remember correctly, we were dancing."

"Dancing?" Anna laughed.

"What? You don't dance anymore? I seem to recall you having some pretty hot moves."

Now it felt as if a frog was trying to clog her windpipe. "No. It's...just been a long time since I've gone dancing."

"Aww. Now that's a shame. Everyone should be able to cut loose every once in a while."

Anna reached up and rubbed her neck as if that would hold her frog back a little longer.

"Anyway," Taariq continued. "We were dancing the salsa."

"The salsa?" She threw her head back. "Now I *know* that you were dreaming."

Taariq started toward her. "The salsa is a very passionate and...a very erotic dance. It's something that I think that you would take to rather easily. If you want...I can even teach you some time."

The frog was back and this time he brought a few friends. Anna coughed and rubbed her neck so hard that Taariq's brows dipped in concern when he stopped in front of her.

"No. I don't think I'll need lessons." She sidestepped around him and damn near ran to the sofa. Surely that would give her enough room to breathe.

Taariq watched her escape with an ever-widening smile. "You were very good...in my dreams."

Anna continued rubbing her neck.

"So good that things got a little heated."

Her gaze leapt over to meet his. "Heated?"

"That's code for X-rated." He sat down on the opposite end of the sofa.

Anna refused to look over at him. Instead, she focused her attention on the small fire she'd started in the fireplace earlier. "You…dreamed about me?"

"Yes."

She waited for him to expand on that but he didn't. Finally her curiosity got the best of her and she turned and looked at him.

"Does that surprise you?" he asked.

"I…" She turned away. "I don't know."

"It shouldn't. And I don't mind admitting that it wasn't my first time."

Her head whipped back around. "It wasn't?"

"No."

Once again, she waited for him to expand on his answers, but it was clear that he wasn't going to fill in the blanks. *How long has he been dreaming about me and what does it mean?* Wait. Wasn't she guilty of the same thing?

"And what about you?"

Despite him asking the question gently, Anna felt like a huge interrogation light just clicked on over her head. She even started squirming in her seat. "What about me?"

Taariq shrugged. "I just confessed to what may have happened on my part, an erotic dream ran wild…but that wouldn't explain your participation."

"Who said that I was a willing participant?" she snapped.

He arched one brow. "You weren't forced," he said flatly but firmly.

"I'm not saying that, either."

"Then what *are* you saying?"

"I'm saying that…that I…"

Taariq cocked his head. "Why can't you admit it?"

"Admit what?" she challenged.

"Who were you dreaming about?"

"No one!"

"Liar."

Anna opened her mouth to respond, but nothing came out and it was her lack of response that was all the answer Taariq needed.

"I'm flattered."

"I wasn't dreaming about you. I don't remember my dreams," she snapped. "Now I don't want to talk about it anymore." She jumped up from the sofa but there was nowhere to go. She was stuck in that cabin for God knows how long with this arrogant ass.

"All right. All right." Taariq sat his cup down on the coffee table. "I didn't mean to upset you."

"You're damn right I'm upset. What you're suggesting is ludicrous. You're the last man I'd fantasize about."

He laughed. "Am I that repugnant to you?"

"To me, yes! In case you haven't been paying attention, I can't stand you!"

Instead of getting angry, Taariq grew more and more amused. "Thanks for clearing that up and, yes, I have been paying attention. I just can't figure out why. Surely you can't be upset about what happened way back—"

Anna stopped pacing and speared him with a contemptuous look. "Can't figure it out?"

He blinked, he couldn't believe how heated she was.

"C'mon." She rolled her eyes back so far that she could practically see behind her. "You can't be that clueless to not know that a woman would be a *little* pissed off that you'd sleep with her and just take off. No note. No phone call." She ticked items off on her hand.

"What?"

He thundered so loud that Anna took a step backward. Out of all his possible reactions, she hadn't expected the complete utter shock that blanketed his face.

Taariq grabbed and shook his head. "What are you talking about? I didn't sleep with you that night!"

Anna's mouth dropped. "How. Could. You. Say. That?"

"Rather easily, thank you very much."

"You don't remember," she said dumbfounded.

"I remember that night rather well. It's you who doesn't remember…which I shouldn't be too shocked by given how much alcohol you had that night."

She closed her mouth…but then tried to open it again, but she still couldn't get her brain to toss out a few words.

Taariq folded his arms. "Let me tell you what *I* remember about that night…"

"Anna?" Another kiss was pressed to her head before there was a gentle shake to arouse her. "Are you awake, baby?"

"Hmm?"

"We're here," Taariq murmured softly and then waited for her response. When he didn't get one, he shook her again. "Baby?"

Anna moaned and then stretched. When her thick fan of lashes opened, she drank in his handsome features. "Hey," she moaned as if waking up to him was completely normal.

Taariq chuckled softly as he shook his head. "Hey, yourself. So you think that you can walk up to your dorm room or should I carry you?"

She snuggled closer. "Like if we were on our honeymoon?"

"Uh…oookay," Taariq hedged. "Exactly how much did you drink tonight?"

Anna rolled her eyes while her smile slid wider. "Oh, I don't know. A couple?"

His laughter deepened. "Just a couple?"

"Something like that." She twirled a finger in her hair as

she finally pulled herself out from under his arm. "Should we go up?"

Taariq's brows arched upward. "Do you think that you can make it?"

She frowned at the silly question. "What do you mean? I'm fine."

He gave her a dubious look but then pulled the keys out of the ignition and climbed out of the car. Since she was practically in his seat, he offered a hand to help her out from his side, as well.

"Whoo," Anna said, almost tumbling.

Taariq kept an arm wrapped around her waist. "Are you sure that you're okay?"

Anna righted herself by clinging to him. "Yeah. Never better." She giggled for a moment and then became fixated on his mouth again. She lifted her finger and then lazily brushed it across the bottom. "I want to kiss you again," she whispered.

Still highly amused, Taariq laughed while he maneuvered to shut his SUV's door behind her.

"Mmm-hmm." She bobbed her head like a little girl.

"You're adorable, do you know that?"

Her smile melted as she dropped her gaze. "Adorable... but not beautiful."

Taariq took hold of her chin and lifted it until their eyes met. "You're both. Beautiful and adorable." He kissed the tip of her nose. "I'm sure you already knew that."

Anna shook her head.

There was a shuffle of feet somewhere before someone shouted, "Y'all get a room somewhere. Damn!"

Taariq smiled against her lips before pulling back. "Let's get you to your room."

"That sounds like a plan," she said.

He just smiled as he walked and supported her with his arm still wrapped around her waist. She did pretty well

*if you ignored her inability to walk in a straight line, and
she seemed to catch a serious case of the giggles halfway
up to her dorm room. When she got her door open, Taariq
took his cue to pull away. "Maybe I can call and check on
you tomorrow?"*

*Anna's face twisted in disappointment. "You're leav-
ing?"*

*"Yeah." He reached up and brushed a lock of hair away
from her face. "I think you need to get a good night's
sleep."*

*"Nooo." She tugged him into the small room by his
shirt. "I want you to stay," she purred.*

*"Trust me. I'd love to stay. But I don't think that's really
a good idea."*

*"Oh, really?" She kicked the door shut and started
pulling up his shirt. "I thought that you wanted to see
some of my other moves. Anna started swaying her hips.
Once she got started, that shining glint returned to his
dark gaze.*

*She kicked off one pump—maybe a little too hard
because it flew high up in the air and smacked Taariq
against his temple.*

"Ow!"

*"Oh." She slapped her hands across her mouth. "I'm
so sorry."*

*Taariq rolled his eyes toward to the door like he was
reconsidering his exit.*

*Anna lowered her hands and redoubled her awkward
seduction show. However, this time she just leaned over to
remove her other shoe. Problem with that was she was still
a little off-balance, so when she leaned…she kept falling
in that direction.*

*"Whoa! Watch it!" Taariq lunged forward, but unfor-
tunately when she made a desperate grab for him, she just*

succeeded in pulling him down with her. She hit the floor.
"Anna? Are you all right?"

"Hmm?"

*He laughed. "You're wasted. C'mon. Let me help you
get into bed."*

*It was a struggle to get her back onto her feet, but
somehow he managed. She dropped her head on his
shoulder and started mumbling something about not
wanting to be a good girl. He just nodded and unzipped
and peeled her out of her dress. Next, he pulled back the
covers and then eased her down onto the pillow.*

*She was still mumbling something when he pulled the
sheet and blanket on top of her. She really was adorable
and beautiful. It was just too bad that she was also drunk.
Taariq shook his head, but couldn't resist pressing one last
kiss to her cheek. "You'll thank me for this in the morning,"
he said. With that, he stood up and left the dorm with Anna
moaning and tossing in her sleep.*

"And that's was the last time we talked until your sister's
wedding."

Anna stared at him in shock. "That's not…I…think that
I need to sit down." She walked back over to the sofa and
then folded over with her face inside her hands. "But…I
remember…I could have sworn…" She looked up at him.
"It all seemed so real."

Taariq shook his head. "It didn't happen. You must have
dreamt it."

"A dream," she echoed.

"Just like last night seemed real."

"Last night *was* real," Anna reminded him.

"But we didn't think so at the time."

She fell silent as she continued to rub her head. "I'm
confused. All this time…"

Taariq joined her on the sofa. "I've done some question-
able things in my time. But I would've never forgiven

myself if I'd tried to sleep with you that night. You were pretty out of it. I thought that I'd see you around again, but you and Charlie stopped hanging out and then Roxanne told us that you'd moved out of her dorm. I think I saw you one other time, but you were acting strange so I thought that you were just embarrassed about that night."

"I'm embarrassed now."

"Don't be."

"Oh. And I threw that drink your face." She slapped a hand over her mouth. "I'm so sorry."

"Well...that was interesting...and oddly refreshing."

Anna laughed, but still felt an incredible amount of guilt. She'd believed a lie for *years.*

"So does this mean that we can be friends now?" Taariq asked.

Anna smiled shyly. "I think that I'd like that."

Chapter 20

For three blistering days Anna and Taariq remained snowed-in in their small cabin on Powder Mountain. They had long ago stopped looking outside the window because there was nothing but a wall of snow. Two days earlier the phone lines went down and the temperature in the cabin was steadily falling, despite the constant fire they had going in the fireplace. To ward off cabin fever, they stayed huddled close to the stone hearth, munching on Spam and crackers and drinking gallons of hot cocoa.

They shared stories and talked about everything—except for what happened that first night he'd arrived.

"Your father took you to a prostitute?" Anna laughed, shaking her head.

Taariq shrugged but his cheeks darkened with a blush of embarrassment. "What can I say? I was a late bloomer and my father thought I needed a little help getting comfortable around the ladies."

"Oh, my God." Anna dropped her face into the palms

of her hands. "I thought that sort of thing only happens in teenage-angst movies."

He shook his head. "I don't know what to tell you. My father was a different kind of cat—the proverbial rolling stone."

"Wherever he laid his hat was his home?"

"Exactly." Taariq's gaze turned reflective. "I idolized him growing up. No matter where we moved to, he was always the coolest brother on the block. Not to mention the women loved him. At one point I thought I had enough aunties to make the Guinness Book of World Records."

"Aunties?"

He laughed. "That's how my father would always introduce his newest girlfriend. *'T, my man. Come and meet your Auntie Pam—or Auntie Theresa',*" he mimicked his father. "I have to admit, they all treated me like a king—primarily because they thought it would get them brownie points with my old man."

"So you were raised with a lot of different women spoiling you?"

"Now I wouldn't say spoiling," he hedged.

"No? What would you call it?"

Taariq's mouth flapped, while his shoulders jumped around. "I'd say that I brought out their natural maternal instincts. I needed it since my mother wasn't around."

"Why not?"

"Because she didn't have any maternal instincts. I suspect that she left me with Dad before he could do the same to her." He shrugged his shoulders. "She left when I was three and I never saw her again."

"I'm sorry."

"Don't be. It was a long time ago." A brief silence hung between them. "So where were we?"

"Your father took you to a prostitute."

"Oh, yeah. Pops thought that if I had sex at least once that it would get the ball rolling."

"How old were you?"

Now his whole face was darkening. "Seventeen."

"That's a good age."

"That's late for a boy. Trust me."

"Really?" Her brows stretched.

"Oh, yeah. Most of my friends lost theirs like at twelve and thirteen. I was teased mercilessly through junior high and high school. It got so bad that I started to lie about it."

"Nooo." Anna laughed.

"Yep. My first girlfriend was this imaginary girl, named Janet—named after Janet Jackson whom I was madly in love with back in the day. Anyway, I told everyone that the reason that they didn't see her around was because she went to some private school out in the suburbs and that her father didn't like her hanging around inner-city kids."

"You put some thought into it," she said, impressed.

"Desperate times called for desperate measures." He chuckled, remembering. "It was crazy trying to keep up with all the lies I had going with the whole Janet affair."

"I just can't imagine you having to resort to lying about a girlfriend. I'd figure you had girls throwing themselves at your feet."

"Nah. Only Kappa brother I imagine I could've hung out with back then would've been Stanley. But don't you tell him."

Anna crossed her heart. "It'll be our little secret."

"Good. I appreciate that."

She hugged her legs tight and then peeked at him over her knees. "Sooo…how was it with the hooker?"

"Awful!" His laughter filled the room.

"You're kidding!" Anna developed a serious case of the giggles.

Taariq shook his head. "I wish I was. My father sent me in with a pack of condoms to become a man and I came out crying like a baby."

"Oh, now you *have* to tell me."

"Her name was Sheila. She was at least two times my age and had a thing for spandex and bamboo earrings. Thick girl—nice smile. She tried to talk to me. Asked me how old I was, what school did I go to? I couldn't get my mouth to work. The whole thing was over in less than a minute and that's all you're going to get out of me."

Anna clutched her side as she continued laughing.

"So glad that I amuse you," he said with a flat smile.

"It's just so…so…pathetic."

"Trust me. I know." They shared another laugh while their gazes drifted over to the fire.

"What about you?" Taariq asked.

"Me?"

"Yeah, you. How was your first time?"

She hesitated.

"C'mon. I told you about Janet and Sheila so come out with it."

"All right." Anna huffed. "I was sixteen."

"Sixteen?" He blinked. "See? Even you beat me."

"What do you mean *even me?*"

"You know what I mean, Ms. Prim and Proper. You were doing the do a whole year before me."

"What's a year?"

"It's an eternity when you're a teenager."

She laughed. "I have to agree with you there."

He waited, and then, "Sooo? Who was it with?"

"Just a boy."

"Janet and Sheila." He rolled his hand. "I'm going to get it out of you."

"All right. It was this guy named Fred."

"Fred?" Taariq frowned. "Sounds like a loser."

"He *wasn't* a loser. He was my biology lab partner." She smiled. "I used to love watching how he would dissect things. I thought he had great hands—and I was right. He went on to become a neurosurgeon."

"Great," Taariq deadpanned.

"He was sensitive and smart."

"Oh, God. I think that I'm going to barf."

"What? You asked."

"My bad. Go on. How did Mr. Surgeon finally make his move?"

Anna dropped her gaze. "Actually, I'm the one that jumped him."

"What?"

She shrugged and avoided his gaze. "What can I say? I was young and impetuous."

Taariq just rolled his hand, impatient for her to get to the nitty-gritty.

"I went to his house so that we could work on our biology paper. When his mother left to run to the store, I sort of just…jumped him."

"Wow. How come you didn't go to my school? I did pretty good in biology."

She blushed. "Oh, God. I can't believe that I told you about Fred."

Taariq tried to ignore a few pinpricks of jealousy about the Fred guy and tried to picture Anna ever doing something so bold. Then again, there was that one night at the frat party. He knew now that night was rare for her. Far as he could tell, she really didn't drink or dress up like a video-vamp often. "So who were you trying to hook up with that night at the frat party?"

Anna's laughter died out. "What?"

He was on to something. "You know. That night, you wore a dress that—wow! But that really wasn't you. I mean that wasn't your style."

"Are you saying that you don't like the way that I dress?"

"I hate it."

"What?"

"C'mon. You have a banging body and you go out of your way to cover it up. I don't get it."

"I don't…"

He cocked his head.

"I'm a business professional. I dress accordingly," she defended.

"You're also a woman—a beautiful woman, I might add."

Anna was taken aback by the compliment. "Thank you."

"Mind if I tell you something else?" he asked.

She shook her head.

"That night I took you home?" He paused for a moment. "I've thought about it a lot over the years."

"Really?"

"Yeah." He waited for her gaze to meet his. "I always wondered what that night would've been like had you…"

"Been sober?" She laughed and dropped her gaze again.

"Just a little more sober," he agreed and then allowed another beat of silence to pass again. "I would've made love to you that night. Lord knows that I wanted to."

Suddenly Anna couldn't breath. "You did?"

He nodded. "I still do."

Their eyes connected and despite the chill in the room, their bodies were suddenly infused with a sweltering heat. Anna wasn't aware of him moving but then he was just inches from her face, their breaths mingling together.

"Let me make love to you," he said, cupping her face and drawing her lips to his.

The moment their mouths connected, she fed off him

like a starved woman. He moved forward, which forced her to ease back until she was lying against the soft bear rug. Their hands became a manic frenzy, pulling and tugging layer after layer of clothes from their bodies. Boots, pants and thermal underwear went flying into the air and despite the amount of clothes they had to remove, they were both naked in less than fifteen seconds.

"Oh, Jesus," Taariq moaned, taking in the exquisite artistry of her body. Before now, he'd only dreamed of what she would look like. And those images paled in comparison to the real thing. "I've died and gone to heaven."

"I was just thinking the same thing." Her hands slid up his chest and around his shoulders. Sleek. Beautiful. Powerful. He was all these things and so much more. "Be gentle with me."

Taariq lifted his head and gazed lovingly down at her. "All I want to do is cherish you."

When Anna gazed up at him, she had no problem believing his words. He took his time caressing and stroking her. It was as if he was trying to memorize every inch. Her nipples had never been so hard or ached so deliciously. When his warm tongue slid across their chocolate tips, her body imploded and a low winding hiss streamed from her lips. Encouraged by her response, Taariq twirled, flicked and even nibbled on the soft flesh while his hand roamed south. It glided over her flat belly and then dipped into the soft curls between her legs.

She arched her back and parted her slim legs. He dipped his fingers inside her downy lips and snaked across the base of her clit.

"Ohh." Anna thrashed her head from side to side as orgasmic tremors spread across her body. Taariq shifted his head from one nipple to the other, while his fingers continued to stroke her in a slow and steady pace. In no time, the sounds of her wetness as well as its sweet aroma caused Taariq to be hit with a sudden hunger pang. He wanted—no—needed to taste her. He was convinced that if he didn't do it soon that he would go crazy. With a husky groan, he abandoned her delicious titties and inched down her curvaceous body.

He kissed her thigh. "Open up for me, baby."

Anna pushed away any embarrassment she might have had and reached down between her legs and peeled her pussy open. Taariq's eyes glittered as if a treasure box had been opened and inside all the riches in the world had been revealed to him.

"Oh, God. You're so gorgeous." He slid his arms around each of her thighs and wasted no time diving right in.

The moment his tongue plunged deep into her depths, Anna gasped and her hips came off the ground. Suddenly, everything was too intense. His wicked tongue twirled around her honeyed walls and then pulled out to suck the nectar off her pulsing clit.

Orgasms shot off like bullets from an AK-47. She instinctively tried to inch away from the assault his mouth rained on her, but his muscular arms had her locked in place. She wasn't going anywhere. Around and around her head spun like a toy top. By the time Taariq satisfied his hunger, she was as limp as a rag doll.

"You need a break, baby?" Taariq chuckled as he climbed back up her body.

Anna started to say "yes" when she felt and then saw his long, thick chocolate cock and experienced a hunger pang of her own. "No. I…" She reached for him.

Taariq smiled and then put his hands behind his back so that she could have full access.

Not only was Anna struck by its beauty, but she was equally impressed by how silky smooth it felt bobbing and gliding in her hands. She stroked him slow and steady as a little payback for what he had put her through, but it was a struggle not to start drooling.

Turnabout was fair play, Taariq learned as Anna doled out her own brand of torture. Her hands were so incredibly soft yet firm that he found himself performing all kinds of tricks in his head to prevent him from blasting off too soon. But he was sure that he was giving himself away just by his choppy breathing. Plus, there were a few moans and groans added to the mix, as well.

However, the true test of his sanity came when Anna's hand dipped forward and her mouth stretched open.

"Sweet. Baby. Jesus." He hissed when her mouth sank over the head of his fat cock. Taariq unclenched his hands from behind his head so that he could instead comb them through her thick hair. He was hypnotized watching her lips slide up and down his shaft. Gently, he pumped his hips, setting a rhythm that she was comfortable with. Soon his head started rolling around his shoulders. When he felt a telltale sign of a pending eruption, he finally pulled back and let his cock pop out of her mouth.

"Enough foreplay, baby." He leaned forward, which forced her to ease back until she was on the floor. Their eyes locked as he hooked her legs on his hips. Their past didn't exist and who knew what tomorrow would bring. All that mattered was the here and now. He glided into her slick, tight opening with a long hiss. And when he moved, Anna whimpered and sighed. His strokes were slow and even at first, but it all started feeling way too good to him, and his hips became a hammer.

Faster. Harder. Deeper.

Anna's moans became a cry of ecstasy.

Faster. Harder. Deeper.

Anna started to convulse.

Faster. Harder. Deeper.

She grabbed hold of his shoulders and tried to hold on for dear life.

Faster.

"Oh, God."

Harder.

"I'm coming. I—"

Deeper.

"Ahh..."

They both exploded at the same time. Her musical scream blended beautifully with his Herculean roar, while their minds and bodies vibrated with aftershocks. Taariq gathered her close and rained kisses against her fevered brow until they both drifted off to sleep, happily content.

Chapter 21

For the next three days Anna and Taariq didn't mind so much their small confinement. Sure, the rations where getting low and the temperature in the cabin remained chilly, but at least the snow had stopped and they could hear machines working outside to get things cleared. But in that time, the couple had discovered numerous ways to stay warm.

Besides having sex, they had their share of pillow fights and tickle contests. She had to learn the hard way that Taariq was extremely competitive and sulked if he lost. One of their favorite games was strip poker. Both layered piles and piles of clothes on before they sat down at the coffee table to play. Anna had him stripped completely naked before she had so much as removed a scarf.

"You cheat," he often said before he started to pout.

Best way to shut him up was to take him back to bed. They had tried every position imaginable. Anna's current favorite was being facedown in the center of the bed while

Taariq mounted her from behind. There was just something about the heat that was generated from his broad chest rubbing against her back that put a smile on her face. When Taariq snaked a hand around her hip and played with her clit at the same time, she bit down and screamed into the pillow.

"I'm addicted to you," Taariq admitted, slumping over onto his side and pulling her close. "You're like a drug."

She giggled. "I think that's the first time I've heard that one."

He smiled lazily against her shoulder blade. "I guess there's a first time for everything."

A long silence stretched between them while he pretended to draw on her back and she started thinking about what would happen once they left the cabin. What did all of this mean? Were they a couple now?

In six days they had talked about a lot of things, but hadn't talked about that.

"What's wrong?" Taariq asked, sensing a change in her.

"Nothing," she lied.

He chuckled as he leaned closer to her ear. "Liar."

She shook her head. "You think you know me that well already?"

"I'm a fast learner." He tapped her on the butt. "C'mon. Talk to me."

Anna sighed as she rolled over so that she could face him. "What's going to happen when we get back to Atlanta?"

He frowned as if he didn't understand the question. "Well. I guess first things first. I'd love to get you into my Jacuzzi." He snuck in for a quick kiss.

"Ha. Ha." She smacked him on his arm. "Be serious. I want to know what's going to happen to us—or, rather, if we're even an 'us.'"

"Oh."

Her brows dipped together at that weird response. "Oh?"

"Well…I, um, haven't really given it that much thought." He pulled back so that he lay against his own pillows.

Anna was stunned by his reaction, but she decided to wait him out while he processed whatever the hell it was that he needed to process.

"Well, of course, I would love to continue seeing you," he said.

"Seeing me?"

"Yeah." He bobbed his head. "I like you."

"Gee. Thanks," she sneered.

"What?" He hunched up his shoulders.

"You want to see me…and other women?"

He hesitated and Anna quickly scrambled off the bed. Taariq sat up. "Wait. Where are you going?"

"Has this past week meant nothing to you?"

"What? Of course it has. We've been having a good time."

"A good time," she repeated and then smacked her hand against her forehead. "I'm just a good time for you?"

"Not just a good time…but, wait, you're twisting my meaning."

"Then just speak plain and tell me what you mean." She folded her arms and stood like an Amazon goddess in front of him.

Taariq didn't know how, but he'd wandered into a minefield. "Whoa. All of this is going so fast."

Anna bobbed her head. "Okay. I get it. We're going too fast for you to consider a monogamous relationship, but we're going at the right pace for us to be screwing like rabbits."

"Monogamous?" He nearly choked on the word.

She shook her head. "I think I'm going to be sick." She took a deep breath, but it didn't stop her from feeling the tears burning in the back of her eyes. Anna turned and stormed toward the bathroom. "Don't worry about it. You don't have to worry about anything going too fast anymore because I'm putting the brakes on this!"

What did I just do? "Anna, wait!" Taariq hopped out of bed and raced behind her, but of course, she'd locked the door. "C'mon, Anna. Let's finish talking about this."

No answer.

"Anna, don't make me feel like the asshole here."

"You feel like the asshole because you *are* the asshole," she shouted back through the door.

He dropped his head against the door and prayed for patience. "Anna, please. I like you. Of course I want to keep seeing you."

No answer.

Taariq placed his ear against the door. "Are you crying?"

"No! I'm not!"

She would've been more convincing if her voice hadn't cracked. Taariq's heart squeezed. He'd never meant to cause her any pain. He definitely didn't want things to end between them. That was the last thing he wanted. He liked her—more than liked her. What he'd been feeling these precious few days…well, it scared the hell out of him. But monogamy wasn't in his DNA. His father was a rolling stone and he had followed in his footsteps.

One man. One woman. Was that really something he could do?

The bathroom door jerked open and Anna shot past him so fast, it stunned him. She quickly grabbed some clothes and headed back.

Taariq blocked the door. "Anna, please. Talk to me."

Without missing a beat, she shoved her weight up against his side. Surprised by her sudden superhuman strength, he went careening sideways while she stormed back into the bathroom and slammed the door shut.

Riiiing! Riiiing!

Taariq jumped at the sudden sound of the telephone ringing. The phone lines were working. He made one step toward the phone, but then Anna bolted back out of the door and raced to answer it.

"Hello."

"Anna, thank God. We've been so worried about you. Management just called and said that they expected everything to be cleared out by late this evening. Charlie and I are dying to get out of here. I miss my baby." She sounded tired. "How are things over there?"

"No murder scene, but I'm like you. I can't wait to get the hell out of here."

Taariq expelled a frustrated sigh behind her.

"So you think you could be ready to go…say, around seven?"

"Girl, I could be ready in five minutes."

"So I assume that you and Taariq are still at each other's throats?" She sounded disappointed.

"You assumed correct."

"Oh, well. We'll see you this evening."

Anna quickly hung up the phone and then glared frostily over at Taariq. "Good news. We'll be back home in Atlanta by tonight and we can go back to our separate lives."

Chapter 22

One month later...

The alarm clock blared in Taariq's ears, insisting that it was time for him to get out of bed. It really meant it this time because he'd hit the snooze button at least ten times already. Groaning, he lifted his head from underneath the bottom of a pile of pillows and swung his arm out to shut off the alarm. But still he flopped his head back down.

He didn't want to get up so he lay there and tried to think of another plausible excuse that he could tell his secretary at the law firm. He would have to tell them something since he hadn't been back to the office since his trip to Utah.

Utah. Anna.

Longing stirred within him along with a growing feeling of emptiness. Taariq pressed a hand against his chest and tried to rub away a maddening ache. Maybe he was coming down with something?

Riiiing! Riiiing!

"Go away," Taariq groaned. He hadn't come up with a good lie yet. The call was switched to the answering machine and suddenly Hylan's voice rang out from the small speaker.

"Yo, T, man! Pick up!" Pause. "C'mon, dude. I know that you're there. Don't make me and the boys come and get you. You're not going to like that, man." During the next pause, Hylan huffed out a long, frustrated breath. "Look. I know that you're hurting. I'm not saying that I know all the details. But, uh, the guys and I have pretty much put two and two together. Since Anna…"

Taariq's head cocked to the speaker. *Since Anna what?*

"Look. I'm just saying that if you need someone to talk to, me and your boys are here for you, man." Pause. "All right then. I guess I'll see you on the flip side. It's Saturday so you know where I'm headed. Peace." Hylan disconnected the call.

Taariq frowned. "Saturday?" He plopped back against the pillows with a wave of relief. He didn't have to go to work after all. Heaving a sigh, Taariq slowly turned his head toward the drawn window and just stared. It was time to be honest with himself. He missed Anna Jacobs. More than he'd missed anyone or anything in his entire life.

Ever since they'd returned to Atlanta she'd refused to take his calls, respond to text messages or even emails. He'd tried pumping Charlie, his so-called brother, for information about what was going on with her, but that was like getting water from a rock. His allegiance was clearly with Anna since she was part of his family now.

Why didn't you tell her that you wanted to be monogamous? he asked himself for the billionth time. Why had he been so afraid to just lay it on the line and just go for it? It was what he felt. How he still felt.

He emitted another longwinded groan. How did he screw this up? And how much longer could this pain in his heart last?

An hour later, Taariq had managed to pull himself together enough to shower and head down to the place where he knew that he could get good advice: Herman's Barbershop.

"Yo, T!" boys in the shop shouted when he strolled through the doors.

He tried to put on a half smile, but Herman's face twisted into a frown. "Man, you look like hell," he stated bluntly.

"Don't you say the nicest things?"

Hylan and Derrick looked up from their chairs and their faces matched the old man's.

"He ain't lying," Derrick said. "You're not sick, are you?"

"I'm something." He eased into a vacant chair and huffed out a long breath.

Hylan smiled. "Well, I'm just glad you finally got out of your house. Good seeing you among the living, man."

"Thanks."

Herman shook his head. "If you ask me, it looks like you have a lot on your mind. Is there something that you want to talk about?"

Taariq's first instincts were to deny everything. "Nah, everything is cool." But to his surprise, Herman just shrugged his shoulders.

"All right." He went back to edging the brother's hair in his chair.

Taariq didn't think the old man would've given up so easily. Now he was stuck trying to ease into the topic he wanted to discuss, so of course, his transition was a bit awkward. "So, um, there's this one girl." He cleared his throat.

Herman smiled. "Yes? Someone you like?"

Taariq bobbed his head. "Yeah. I'm, um, really feeling her a lot—only, I think I may have really screwed things up."

"Oh?"

So far, so good. He cleared his throat again. "Pretty much. I sort of told her that I didn't do monogamous relationships. Well, I didn't say it really. I sort of reacted pretty badly and…"

"You wish that you could do a do-over?" Herman filled in the blanks for him.

Taariq dropped his gaze. "Yeah."

"Been there done that." Herman chuckled.

A number of dudes started nodding.

"Let me ask you something. Do you love her?"

Taariq pulled in a deep breath while every eye in the place zoomed over to him. But there was no more denying the truth, not since he'd spent the last month in bed feeling miserable. "Yes. I do."

"Aww. I *told* you, man!" J.T. threw up a hand and proceeded to collect a round of high fives.

Everyone's face exploded with smiles and a few of the dudes shouted out congratulations or moaned in despair.

Bobby, who was working Hylan's hair, started laughing. "Man, you Kappa boys are falling one by one—aren't you? Derrick, Charlie, Hylan and now you. Next thing you're going to tell me is that Stanley's going to get hitched. Shoot, we can't even call him Breadstick no more since he done pumped up."

The bell above the door jingled and Charlie and Stanley strolled in.

"Speak of the devil," Bobby said. "Looks like someone is out of their cast."

Taariq and Stanley's eyes crashed. There was an instant flash of anger in Stanley's blue eyes as he sailed across the room. Taariq stood and put his hands up in the air. "Wait, Stanley. Let me explain." That was all that he got out before Stanley sent his fist flying across his jaw. He head snapped to the side and stars exploded behind his eyes.

"Whoa!" Brothers jumped out of their seats, but it was Charlie and Derrick who grabbed hold of Stanley and pulled him back.

"Let's get something straight," Stanley roared. "We ain't brothers and we ain't friends—you got that?!"

Taariq reined in his initial instincts to fight back and just glared at Stanley.

Stanley fought for his release and snapped at the other Kappa brothers. "Get off me!"

They looked at each other and then slowly released him. Everyone watched to see what he would do next, but he just gave Taariq a parting glare and stormed out of the shop.

After a beat of silence, everyone started buzzing around the shop.

"Are you all right?" Charlie asked.

Taariq tested his jaw and then nodded. "Yeah. I'm cool."

Herman folded his arms and shook his head. "You really did screw up."

Taariq huffed out a long breath. "Tell me something I don't know."

"How about I just tell you how to get your woman back?"

"Uh-oh." Bobby shook his head. "It looks like someone is about to turn in their player's card."

"So let me get this straight," Emmadonna said, scratching the side of her head. "You dreamed that you slept with him in college and then slept with him while you thought you were dreaming? Did I get that right?"

"I'm afraid so," Anna said, folding her arms. She had

kept all of this inside for so long that it finally just exploded out of her. For the first time in a long while, she was the center of discussion at their Lonely Hearts book club.

"So you guys were just…screwing for about a week in the mountains?" Jade said in awe. "You and Taariq Bryson? That fine son of—"

"Jade," Ivy snapped. "We get the picture."

Anna sucked in a deep breath. "You know it was just a big mistake. I mean, I should've known better. He's a Kappa."

Jade shrugged. "Yeah, but they're starting to marry off. That has to be a little encouraging. If they can start settling down then there's still hope."

Emmadonna frowned. "I don't think that you're helping."

The doorbell rang and Anna started to get up.

"Don't you move," Em said. "I'll get it. You sit right there. I'll play hostess today."

Anna smiled even though she just wanted them all to leave so that she could go back to bed.

Emmadonna swished her hips toward the door, thinking that she was just going to let Gisella in. After all, she'd been popping up at their meetings a lot lately. Never in her wildest imagination did she expect to see Taariq's fine butt leaning against the door frame.

"Oh, I'm sorry," he said frowning. "I thought that this was Anna Jacobs's apartment." He cocked his head. "Wait. Don't I know you?"

Em just blinked up at him.

"Hello?" he asked.

"Emmadonna, who's at the door?" Anna shouted.

Taariq perked up. "Excuse me." He stepped around Emmadonna and strolled toward the living room. He stopped when he saw the room filled with women. "Good morning, ladies."

Anna's head jerked up and a second later, her mouth fell open. "Taariq?" She blinked. "What are you doing here?"

He smiled and then noticed that every eye was on him. "I came to talk to you."

Anna slowly stood up from her chair while she shook her head. "I think that we said all that we needed to say at—"

"I love you," he blurted out.

Anna blinked. "What?"

"I thought that would get your attention." He smiled and moved toward her.

"You can't just show up here and say something like that." She started circling the other way. "What am I supposed to say to that?"

"I don't know." He shrugged. "That you love me, too? And if you don't...I can wait. I'll wait a lifetime if you want. I just know that I can't..." He huffed out a long breath and shook his head. "I just know that I can't go back to living without you."

The circle of women gasped and then swung their eyes back toward Anna whose eyes were as huge as boulders.

"What?" It was all that she could think to say. "You can't... I can't..."

"Yes, we can." He reached into his pocket and pulled out a black velvet box.

Another gasp went up.

Anna's knees wobbled. "I have to be dreaming again," she whispered. "This can't be happening."

Taariq stopped before her and knelt down. "Anna Jacobs, I've known you a long time and I've thought...and *dreamed* about you a lot over the years. I didn't know what it truly was that I felt for you until I saw you again all these years later. But even then I've struggled and fought to put a name for what I was feeling inside. The thought of really losing you or even seeing you with another man may have cost me a longtime friend."

She frowned in confusion.

"I have to stop running and fighting," he resumed saying. "That week in the cabin was the most beautiful experience I've ever known and I was a fool—a proud and scared fool. I didn't mean to hurt you. I love you and I know as sure as I'm kneeling before you that I'll always love you. Will you marry me?" He opened the box and revealed a beautiful two-carat, emerald-cut diamond.

Anna stared at him in shock while a heavy silence lapsed between them. Vaguely she was aware of her girls grabbing and holding on to one another. But all she could think and feel were these wonderful emotions churning inside of her.

"Yes," she whispered a second before tears rushed to her eyes and blurred her vision. "Yes, I'll marry you."

The women squealed, screamed and jumped around as if they were all the latest Mega Millions lottery winners.

A smile exploded across Taariq's face as he removed the ring from the box and slipped it onto her finger. A perfect fit. He stood up and then swept his newly bejeweled fiancée into his muscular arms. "I swear that you'll never regret this."

"I know," she whispered and then leaned up against his tall frame to seal their promise with a kiss.

* * * * *

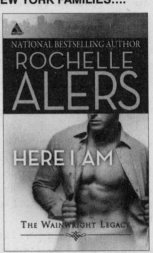

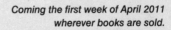

REQUEST YOUR FREE BOOKS!

2 FREE NOVELS
PLUS 2 FREE GIFTS!

KIMANI™ ROMANCE

Love's ultimate destination!

KROM11

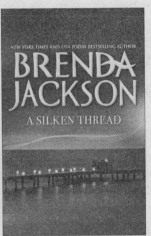